ZOEY DEAN'S
TALENT

ZOeY DeaN'S
TALeNT

razor
bill

Talent

RAZORBILL

Published by the Penguin Group
Penguin Young Readers Group
345 Hudson Street, New York, New York 10014, U.S.A
Penguin Group (USA) Inc., 375 Hudson Street, New York, New York 10014, U.S.A
Penguin Group (Canada), 90 Eglinton Avenue East, Suite 700, Toronto, Ontario,
Canada M4P 2Y3 (a division of Pearson Penguin Canada Inc.)
Penguin Books Ltd, 80 Strand, London WC2R 0RL, England
Penguin Ireland, 25 St Stephen's Green, Dublin 2, Ireland
(a division of Penguin Books Ltd)
Penguin Group (Australia), 250 Camberwell Road, Camberwell, Victoria 3124,
Australia (a division of Pearson Australia Group Pty Ltd)
Penguin Books India Pvt Ltd, 11 Community Centre, Panchsheel Park,
New Delhi–110 017, India
Penguin Group (NZ), Cnr Airborne and Rosedale Roads, Albany, Auckland 1310,
New Zealand (a division of Pearson New Zealand Ltd)
Penguin Books (South Africa) (Pty) Ltd, 24 Sturdee Avenue, Rosebank,
Johannesburg 2196, South Africa

Penguin Books Ltd, Registered Offices: 80 Strand, London WC2R 0RL, England

10 9 8 7 6 5 4 3 2 1

alloy**entertainment**

Produced by Alloy Entertainment
151 West 26th Street
New York, NY 10001

Library of Congress Cataloging-in-Publication data is available

Printed in the United States of America

For Kerry—
I couldn't have done it without you!

ZOEY DEAN'S
TALENT

chapter
one

◄ Tuesday   September 1 ►

10:45 AM	Outfit selection for premiere party (prelim. round)
11 AM	GPS to M Café
12 PM	Outfit selection for premiere party (semifinals)
12:30 PM	Last-min. tanning, SPF 30
1:30 PM	Model outfits with new glow (final round)
4 PM	Confirm Becks's ETA
6 PM	Check Coco's flight stats
9 PM	Premiere! Inner Circle reunion at Teddy's! BNE (BEST NIGHT EVER!)

Mackenzie Little-Armstrong held her iPhone high above her golden-blond head, pouted, and snapped a self-portrait. She needed to cross-check her outfit. Mirrors could lie. So could camera phones, actually. But they didn't lie at the same time.

Mackenzie, known to family, friends, and much of L.A.'s A-list as Mac, looked down at her camera phone and sighed at the evidence.

Purr-fection.

She was wearing a white sundress that she'd just had flown in from her favorite store in Paris, Stella Forest, with caramel-colored sandals that revealed her pale pink pedicure. She'd shimmered her eyelids with a white M·A·C (of course!) powder that made her turquoise eyes just a tad brighter, and polished off her look with super-black mascara. She looked effortlessly cute, which of course took the most effort of all.

Mac admired her image at arm's length, her signature wooden bangles sliding down her tan arms, when her phone rang. It was Becks's 310 cell number, which meant *The Evangelina*—the jet MTV superstar Clutch Becks had named after his only daughter—had touched down in California. Mac yanked the phone to her ear, all seven wooden bracelets clunking to her elbow.

"Becks, you're back!" Mac squealed. Becks spent every summer surfing in Oahu with her dad, and it had been eighty-three days since Mac had last seen her. "Don't ever leave me again," Mac added melodramatically. "I *caaaan't* wait to see you."

"I know!" Becks shouted so loud Mac had to hold the phone an inch from her diamond-studded ear. "T minus five hours. I see we have plans for tonight." She laughed. Mac and her two best friends had synched their iPhones so that they could always keep track of one another. Or, more precisely, so Mac could keep track of her friends and let them know where to be and when. Tonight, Mac had invited Becks and their other BFF, Cordelia Kingsley, better known as Coco, to a red-carpet premiere party for Davey Woodward's newest movie, *Sea Devils*.

Davey was The Next Big Thing, and Mac's mother, Adrienne Little-Armstrong, was his agent.

"But I have *nothing* to wear," Becks fake-whined.

"Well, Becks, on a scale of one to ten, how tan are you?" Mac asked, picking up her copy of French *Vogue* for inspiration. Becks had strawberry-gold hair and golden skin, and every summer she returned to SoCal just a tad more golden. Mac had to factor this into her BFF's outfit selection. It was a science, really.

"If I was a four in June," Becks said thoughtfully, "now I'm a six."

"Perfect." Mac closed the magazine with a quick flick of the wrist. "Wear your Marni sundress with those Jimmy Choo ballet flats I told you to buy at South Coast Plaza." Mac smiled in satisfaction. She needed to be needed the way other girls needed oxygen. Or, in the case of Beverly Hills girls, the newest Chloé bag.

"Done!" Becks said gratefully.

Mac eased into her pale green Louis XIV sofa chair and sipped her frothy soy latte, courtesy of Berta, the Armstrongs' housekeeper. She flipped through a stack of postcards she'd received that week: Bali. St. Moritz. Ile de Ré. Toyko. Maui. As she dropped the pile into her blue fleur-de-lis Pierre Deux letter box, her eyes landed on her advance copy of *People* magazine. She got every celebrity weekly before they were released to the general public—being the daughter of Hollywood royalty had its perks.

"Have you heard from Coco?"

"Her plane lands any minute now," Mac said. Coco had texted Mac from the runway in London to say she'd be approximately seventeen minutes late touching down. Mac loved that, despite a summer apart, she was still the information hub. Information—as everyone in Hollywood knew—was power. She licked her finger and began flipping the glossy pages of *People*. There were post-pregnancy pictures of Nicole. Brad and the latest baby in Venice. Ashlee and Jessica at the beach.

And then Mac saw *it*.

"Code red!" Mac said, almost dropping her iPhone. She spilled some latte on her dress from shock. "Guess who's on page forty-three of next week's *People*?" Mac didn't wait for a response. "My entire family. The article is called *Hollywood's Uber-Family*."

"What's wrong with that?"

There were so many things wrong with *that*, Mac didn't know where to begin. "I'm not even *in* the family photo!" The photo showed her parents,

Lanyard and Adrienne; her older brother, Jenner; and her younger sister, Maude. *Like she didn't even exist.*

But it wasn't just that, Mac realized, scanning the caption. While Jenner was described as "fifteen, a Billabong-sponsored surf star," and Maude was "ten, a certified genius," and her father was "the Academy Award–winning screenwriter," and her mother was "Hollywood's most powerful agent, a partner at Initiative," Mac was just . . ."(not pictured), twelve, an eighth-grader at the Bel-Air Middle School."

Like it was an *accom*plishment to go to middle school.

It was a particularly sensitive topic for Mac because she had tried desperately, secretly, to find a talent. A familiar mental slide show began running through her mind of her many failed attempts at finding something to call her own:

1. GOLF: Bo-ring! Cute outfits, though.
2. SWIMMING: Who knew you could get disqualified for wearing a Marni bikini to a meet?
3. BALLET: Pedicure disaster.
4. TANGO: Jacob Spaghetti-Arms for her partner? No, *gracias*.

5. VOICE: Possibly tone-deaf.
6. DRAMA: Kimmie T's territory. Plus, Mom uses failed actors' headshots as bedding for Maude's Ecuadorian hamster, Jorge.
7. CREATIVE WRITING: The last thing in life Mac wanted was a reason to be all alone.
8. SOCCER: Ball kicked at face = swollen nose = no.

The problem with all of the activities—since apparently Mac had no natural talent for any of them—was that in order to get *good* you first had to be *bad*. And Mac didn't love anything enough to risk looking ridiculous for it.

"Who cares about *People*?" Becks asked, snapping Mac out of her self-pitying reverie. Becks had never understood popularity, because she'd never had to work for hers. She was naturally gorgeous and athletic, and had the body of a Roxy girl. "Hello? You're about to be elected social chair. You'll *officially* rule BAMS—as if you don't already."

Social chair was the most coveted position at BAMS, a.k.a. Bel-Air Middle School, because it basically meant being elected a school-wide VIP. The SC represented the student body to the administration on all things fun. She (and yes, she was *always* a she) picked performers at school dances (Justin T? Check!) and made recommendations to the school cafeteria (soy lattes? Double-check). One year the SC even chose new gym uniforms (bringing Burberry plaid minis back? Check plus!).

"How can I win social chair if I'm a loser in a national magazine?" Mac already knew the answer to that. Elections took place the first week of the school year, which meant the first days of school were *crew-shal*.

"Yeah, but—"

Mac was too frustrated to listen. She wanted to throw her latte at her Tiffany-blue wall, but she loved her perfectly planned bedroom too much to get coffee stains everywhere. Instead, she carefully set her latte down on her white Saarinen side table. "Becks, sorry to bounce, but I need to get into this with Mama Armstrong. Au revoir."

"Aloha," Becks said. "See you tonight!"

Mac didn't hear the "See you tonight" because she'd already begun storming downstairs to the study, where her mother was working from home, despite the fact that it was a bright summer afternoon. Mac knew better than to interrupt when her mother was on the phone, but this was an emergency.

"Talk to me," Adrienne barked.

"My life is ruined!" Mac cried.

"I'm a talent agent, not a magician!" Adrienne picked up a snow globe from Paris and looked as if she might be about to fling it at the ecru walls, then thought better of it and put it down. The glitter inside sparkled around the Eiffel Tower. Mac realized her mother wasn't speaking to her.

Adrienne was "rolling calls," which meant that one of her three assistants had to get A-listers on the phone and transfer them to Adrienne, who did not do normal things, like dial phone numbers.

"I don't have an all-American girl who can act like an all-American boy. And yes, I agree that Anastasia could handle this, but unfortunately I rep every worthwhile Hollywood darling *but* her."

Mac stood in front of her mother's Lucite desk so she could not be ignored. She shifted impatiently on the off-white Berber rug and examined the ends of her blond hair, which stretched all the way down to her back.

"What do you want me to say?" Adrienne said into the headset. "If the studio is serious, they'll go to every mall in Middle America and say *Deal with It* is the role of a lifetime opposite Davey Woodward.

Otherwise, it's not gonna happen, Elliot." She sighed. "So deal with *that*."

Adrienne hung up the phone and swiveled in her Aeron chair to face her daughter. Adrienne had a tiny, heart-shaped face with a pointy chin and pointy cheekbones, and a reddish-blond bob that curled under. If you didn't know better, you might describe her as sweet-looking. "Mackenzie, promise me you will never become an agent."

Mac sighed. Sometimes she thought it was funny when her mother was melodramatic. Other times, like now, it was not.

"Mom, I need to talk to you about *this*," Mac said, waving the copy of *People* magazine in the air. "Don't you know people at *People*?" Adrienne could do anything with one phone call.

"Mac, not now." Adrienne adjusted her hands-free headset and threw a script into a recycling bin. Mac couldn't believe her mother was acting so nonchalant about something that was going to destroy her. "No one will know how cute I got this summer since I'm not even *in* this article!" she said, careful not to whine, since her mother had a zero-tolerance policy for whining.

This summer, her braces had come off, leaving perfect white teeth. Her blond hair had grown to the middle of her back, plus she was dressing way better, thanks to several meetings with Xochi (pronounced ZO-hee) Dawn, L.A.'s top stylist to the starlets.

"I'm an über-loser in this über-article!" To make her point, Mac tossed the magazine on top of her mom's discarded script in the recycling bin.

Adrienne finally looked at her daughter. She took off her Tina Fey glasses, a sign that her limited patience was about to expire. "Mac. You were at camp, and *People* had a deadline."

It was true. Mac had been at camp all summer. It was called New Adventures, and she'd chosen it specifically for its rotating schedule. Once a week campers were "immersed" in different "unique" activities: glassblowing. Tae kwon do. Parasailing. Mac had hoped something would click, but by the end of each one-week cycle, she was beyond ready to try the next thing. A lot of good camp had done her. But that was so not the point. "Do you understand what this will do to my reputation?" Mac pleaded. "School starts next week, and everyone is going to smile to my face and make fun of me behind my back."

"In Hollywood? Never!" Adrienne pretended to gasp. She put her hands on her cheeks. And then, as if noticing Mac for the first time, Adrienne blinked, then rubbed her temples. "Sweetheart, we live in a dishonest world, which is why we have to be honest with each other." She paused dramatically. "And to be perfectly honest, that skirt is too short. I can't let you leave the house dressed like that."

Mac rolled her eyes and exhaled so that wisps of feathery blond hair blew around her face. "Mom! It's the perfect end-of-summer style *and* fabric." She waved her arms over her white dress for emphasis. "And I *have* to look great tonight to do damage control!"

Adrienne put on her glasses and looked right at Mac, which meant that what she was about to say was nonnegotiable: "Go change."

Mac turned on her caramel-colored kitten heel and sauntered out without another word. Fine, she'd change. And her next outfit would be even better. Her reputation depended on it.

CHAPTER
TWO

Emily & Paige's L.A. Itinerary

Tuesday, September 1

9 AM   Econo Lodge breakfast. Don't load up just cuz it's free! (Celeb Sighting Potential: 0)

11 AM   Universal Studios tour (CSP: 0)

1 PM   Lunch at Universal CityWalk (CSP: 0)

3 PM   Hollywood Wax Museum (CSP: negative 0)

E mily Mungler and her best friend, Paige Harrington, were staring at Davey Woodward's shiny black hair and dimpled chin. They were oblivious to the fact that Emily's mother, Lori Mungler, was snapping pictures of their magical moment.

"It's so great to finally meet you," Emily said to Davey, looking right at him with her big brown eyes, her rosy cheeks aglow.

"You're even cuter in person than you are on TV," Paige chimed in. Like Emily, she also had apple-red cheeks, but she had frizzy brown hair and tiny Renée Zellweger eyes. At Cedartown Middle School, where Paige and Emily would soon be eighth-graders, people said (not to her face, of course) that Paige was a slightly less cute and slightly fatter version of Emily. They also said that Emily was snobby and aloof (not to her face, either). Really Emily was just a little shy and very pretty and didn't care *all* that much about what other kids thought. Which of course only made *them* care more about *her*.

Emily ran her fingers through her wavy cinnamon-brown hair, which had streaks from where she'd tried to turn it blond with Clairol. She pulled it into a side ponytail and leaned in to kiss her crush. She closed her eyes and imagined Davey was just the tiniest bit nervous about kissing *her*.

But before she could even touch his white James Dean T-shirt, alarm bells sounded. The other tourists in the Hollywood Wax Museum glared at Emily and Paige, whose Very Berry–glossed lips were still puckered in Davey's direction.

They were extra-conspicuous because they were both wearing the same outfit: deconstructed-looking blue gingham dresses Paige had sewn and navy Converse minus the shoelaces. They even wore matching word bangle bracelets on their right hands. Emily had one that said, PAIGE IS MY BFF, and Paige's said, EMILY IS MY BFF. The only difference in their outfits was that Emily had a red fake-Gucci purse she'd bought on Hollywood Boulevard minutes earlier.

Emily and Paige were in L.A. for a week's

vacation, and they had decided it would be fun to dress the same every day. Their favorite joke was to tell people they were twins, which was ridiculous, because they obviously weren't. It was one of Paige's many silly schemes devised to make their lives a little funnier.

"You can't touch the statues!" a chubby security guard in a too-tight red blazer yelled. He frantically waved his arms, his jacket lifting up over his protruding stomach, even though the alarms had stopped.

"Sorry, sir," Paige apologized. "We got excited. We love Davey."

"How unusual," the guard mumbled with a smirk.

"No one loves Davey like these two," Lori piped up. She put the disposable camera into her bright purple fanny pack, zipped it shut, and patted it twice for good measure.

Lori had a point. Many thirteen-year-old girls might claim to be obsessed with Davey Woodward and could probably recite the intro-level big duhhhh facts: He was fifteen, the oldest of three boys, raised in Ventura by a single mother, and had a fish named Jack. However, most could not tell you the street name of his first L.A. apartment (Sweetzer), his salary for his first episode of *Just the Five of Us* (eight thousand dollars), his agency (Initiative), or the number of antique cars he owned even though he wasn't old enough to drive (seven).

Paige and Emily had a very high Davey-Q, thanks to hours logged in front of E! Television and years of devouring magazines like *People* and *Us Weekly*. Paige insisted on receiving the inside-Hollywood information because she wanted to be an actress someday and felt she "should know the business," as she would happily tell anyone who asked. Emily simply loved Davey, and compared every boy she met to him. Even his wax likeness surpassed the boys back home.

"We don't have wax museums in Iowa." Lori smiled to the security guard. "We're just so grateful to be here. You know, I put my desire to go to L.A. into the universe and the universe responded." Lori was an emergency room nurse who was totally infatuated with and inspired by self-help books. Currently her favorite was *The Secret*, with some wisdom from *The Tao of Pooh* mixed in.

Emily bit her lip so she wouldn't say anything bratty or seem ungrateful to her mother. After all, Lori had won five thousand dollars in a Fourth of July apple pie bake-off and decided to spend all her earnings to take Emily and her best friend, Paige, on a "fun trip to Los

Angeles." It was just that they had different definitions of a "fun trip to Los Angeles." Emily and Paige knew from *Us Weekly* that stars went shopping on Robertson, not to see themselves in wax.

Emily sighed and gave Davey a parting smile. Even if he was waxen, it was the closest she'd ever been to a real live star.

Emily and Paige sat cross-legged on the orange-and-brown-flecked Econo Lodge motel carpet while they wrote postcards to people in Cedartown. At that moment, Emily was writing "xoxo" on a postcard to her next-door neighbor, Denise. Paige was writing to her parents, Sue and Tom.

The girls had Crest Whitestrips on their teeth and had just doused their lips in Burt's Bees honey-scented lip balm. Yum. It was all part of Paige's pre-eighth-grade improvement plan, which included Clairol to lighten their hair, Jergens Natural Glow to get that *CosmoGirl!* cover-girl tan, and one hundred crunches before bed. "The Plan" was also why Paige was currently setting her bright pink digital swatch for 8 p.m., to remind them to eat Apple Pie Lärabars—they were eating five "mini meals" a day, à la Jessica Alba and Jennifer Aniston. Some people thought Paige was bossy, but Emily loved that her friend made her try new things. Besides, since Paige wanted to be an actress, taking care of her looks was kind of part of the job.

"I'm beat." Lori reclined on the bed and patted her belly. It was six o'clock and they'd just finished their freakishly early dinner. "That time difference really gets to you."

"Mom," Emily whined. Nothing could overcome the sound of Lori's snoring. Not earplugs. Not a TV. Not sending thoughts of silence into the universe. "You *can't* go to sleep now."

"Of course not. I have to wash my face," Lori said, shuffling toward the bathroom. Just before closing the door, she added, "And *then* I can go to sleep!"

Emily shot Paige a look. Just as she was about to make a crack, Emily heard the name Davey Woodward on the TV, and both girls' heads insta-swiveled toward the screen. Davey was being interviewed on the red carpet at Grauman's Chinese Theatre for his new movie, *Sea Devils*. It was about a brave group of deep-sea fishermen who uncover a porthole to hell in the ocean.

Tonight he looked particularly adorable in a black Armani suit with a silver-blue tie that showed off his sky-blue eyes. He ran his fingers through his black hair, which flopped across his forehead and was long enough to tuck behind his ears. He gave all his usual pat answers: He hated to watch his own movies. He was fortunate to work with such talented people. And then Davey said something that made them drop their postcards:

"I'm excited for the after-party at Teddy's."

Paige and Emily's eyes met, reading each other's minds. Teddy's was at the Roosevelt Hotel. The Roosevelt Hotel was one of the trendiest hotels on Hollywood Boulevard, recently redone to restore its 1920s glamour.

"That's like, ten blocks from here," Paige hissed, in her I'm-freaking-out voice.

"We can't afford a cab if we want to get anything at Fred Segal," Emily noted. The girls had saved all their summer babysitting money to buy vintage tees at the coolest clothing store in L.A.

"So we walk," Paige scoffed, pulling her frizzy brown hair into a ponytail. Emily's mind went into a split screen. On one side, she imagined her mom waking up and freaking out that they were gone. On the other side, she imagined meeting Davey Woodward and falling in love at first sight.

"Your mom sleeps through anything," Paige pointed out. "We wait a few hours till she's definitely in REM, and then go. She'll never know."

This was true. Emily tapped her postcard of a wax Hilary Duff. Her mother flushed the toilet in the bathroom.

"Think about it," Paige went on, more urgently now. "We're finally in L.A. and we're watching E!. We may as well be in Iowa. Could you really live with yourself knowing that Davey Woodward was blocks away and you did *nothing*?" Paige emphasized the last word melodramatically.

Emily sat quietly and calculated the risk factor. Getting kidnapped and chopped up in a million pieces by a Los Angeles psycho was definitely a possibility. But so was meeting the boy of her dreams.

"When she snores, we're out." Emily smiled, her pulse already quickening.

Their vacay was finally about to begin.

CHAPTER THREE

becks

◀ Tuesday   September 1 ▶

6 AM	Sunrise surf
7:15 AM	Sayonara, Oahu! Sleep on plane
2 PM	Back on L.A. time/Check in w/Mac
4 PM	Home-turf surf!
9 PM	Premiere at Teddy's. Reunion! BNE!

E vangelina Becks paddled into the surf and inhaled the salty Pacific Ocean smell she loved so much. It was her favorite time of the day: Magic Hour, just before sunset when the Malibu shore was bathed in pink sunlight. The beach was nearly empty, save for a few stragglers playing volleyball or walking their dogs. The gentle ocean swells rocked her silver Al Merrick board.

Before leaving the house, she'd coated her skin in SPF 45 sunscreen so that she wouldn't alter her tan for her best friend's carefully selected outfit choice. Becks wasn't afraid to torpedo down seven-foot waves, but choosing between leopard-print ballet flats and Marc Jacobs wedges stressed her out, especially when she'd spent the summer alternating between the same three bikinis and not giving it a second thought.

In the distance, Becks could see her sprawling,

stucco beach house. It had been a thank-you gift from MTV to her father, Clutch Becks, for earning the network "bajillions of dollars" (as he put it) from his long-running prank show, *That Was Clutch*. Everything in her house was a boy fantasy: an indoor bowling alley, a movie theater, a video game arcade, twisty slides leading from the bedrooms into the deep end of the pool. Becks could literally roll out of bed, hop onto a waterslide, and land in the water.

Massive clouds of gray smoke rose from the patio, and Becks focused on the tiny dots in the distance: Her dad and his *That Was Clutch* cohorts were grilling. She heard a *pop* and then hysterical laughter, and watched as one of her dad's friends ran into the house holding his nose.

Ever since her mom died when she was a baby, it had been her and her dad in that huge house. They'd started spending even more time together two years ago, when Clutch had retired after a near-death incident with an angry armadillo and decided to "change his lifestyle." He still had his friends over all the time, but the difference now was that he fed them organic veggie burgers instead of kicking them in the crotch. Usually.

She paddled closer to the crest of a wave that was about to break and ducked inside, just in time to ride it all the way to the shore. Climbing onto the beach, she wedgie-checked her Quiksilver bikini and shook the salt water out of her ear by turning her head sideways and hopping on each foot.

"Looking good out there, Becks."

She turned to see her next-door neighbor and best guy-friend, Austin Holloway, smiling at her. Becks planted her board in the sand and ran full speed ahead, like a freckled cannonball. She wasn't one for formal hellos.

"*Ooof*," Austin said as she barreled into him. The volleyball players looked over curiously and then returned to their game.

"Why aren't *you* in the water?" she asked as she righted herself post-tackle. She stood and grinned at him. Something was . . . different about Austin. Actually, *everything*. She had to *crane* her neck to look him in the face. His sandy, sun-streaked brown hair was long and shaggy and fell over his eyebrows. His arm muscles — *arm muscles?* — pressed out of his black Hurley T-shirt.

"I didn't want to get shown up out there," he said, swatting her arm with his ratty blue surf towel. "You're a rock star!"

Becks grinned. Mac and Coco sometimes hung out on the beach to rate Becks's maneuvers like in a real surfing competition, but they didn't understand the sport. (Bad facial expression—minus two! Wedgie—minus fourteen!) "Oh, you know . . . I've been practicing," she told him faux-bashfully.

He laughed. "So when'd you get back? You see the *ick* yet?"

"If you mean Mac and Coco, I'll see them tonight," she told him, grabbing his towel and throwing it up the sand ridge. Austin called the Inner Circle the I.C. He also happened to pronounce it *ick*.

"First one to grab the towel wins!" he cried, running up the seaweed-dotted dune. It was one of their oldest games, invented after their secret flashlight language and after Austin had officially beaten her in their thumb-wrestling championship.

She kicked up sand as she went, startling a passing old lady and her wiener dog, who scowled at them. Becks was about to win when all of a sudden she felt two strong arms envelop her. Austin threw her down and she tumbled to the sand on her back.

"Just because you can officially surf better than me doesn't mean you can beat me in towel-football!" Austin said, pinning her against the sand, holding her hands next to her ears.

Becks squirmed so her right cheek was on the dry, sandy grass. She could hear her heart in her ears.

Normally she would have fought him off, but this time, when he came closer, Becks didn't push him away. Even when she felt his breath touch her left cheek, she forgot the shove she was supposed to give him. And then . . .

He licked her.

"Nasty!" He flicked his tongue like he'd just tasted liver.

As if snapping back to life, Becks remembered how she usually behaved in this situation. "Gross, Holloway!" she cried, pushing him up off of her.

"Victory!" he yelled, grabbing the towel and holding it over his head. He did a little end-zone line dance and tossed his floppy brown hair out of his thickly lashed eyes. "Anyway, gotta get some eats with Moms. Welcome home, sucka!" He started to jog back toward his house, leaving Becks lying there, her back pressed against the cool, early evening sand.

Becks reached up to feel her level-six-tanned cheek with her right hand. She tenderly touched the spot where Austin's tongue had brushed her skin.

Technically it was a lick. A nasty, run-of-the-mill lick from Austin. It involved *saliva*.

So why on earth, Becks wondered, was her heart still pounding?

chapter
Four

COCO

◀ Tuesday   September 1 ▶

9 AM   Breakfast at Kensington Orangery

7:10 PM   LAX at last!

7:30 PM   Put on YSL jumbo shades (Mom's picking me up!)

8 PM   Send pics of party outfit selections to Mac

9 PM   Par-tay!!! Reunion!!! BNE!!!

Cordelia Kingsley adjusted her fully reclining seat in the first-class cabin of British Airways flight 1024, nonstop from Heathrow to LAX. Ever since she was a little girl, she had decided to go by the name Coco and spent summers living in the penthouse suites of five-star luxury hotels around the world. Her father, Charles Kingsley, owned the King hotel chain, which meant that Coco knew trendy neighborhoods like SoHo in New York, Avenue Montaigne in Paris, and Aoyama in Tokyo the way other girls knew their local mall. It also meant that Coco had a *lot* of mini soaps engraved with her initials. This summer, she'd stayed with her dad in London while he opened a hotel in Covent Garden.

As the plane approached Los Angeles's sea of twinkling lights, Coco brushed her chocolate-brown hair into a neat ponytail and ran through her checklist of everything she needed to tell her mother. Besides the silly observations she'd sent in her weekly post-cards (McVitie's with Earl Grey tea rocked! Shopping at Harvey Nicks was the best! Black taxis were totally chic), what Coco *really* wanted to talk about with her mother was dancing. Specifically, the dancing she'd learned that summer.

Coco's dream in life was to become a pop star like her über-famous mom. She'd always been a great singer, but her dancing had to improve for Coco to go from downloading iTunes music videos to being *downloadable*.

Which was why her dad opening a new hotel in London had provided the perfect opportunity to train with the world-famous Marcel Marcel. Twenty years earlier, he'd transformed her mom—then a skinny girl from Manchester named Carla with a powerful soprano—into *Cardammon*, the world-famous pop star.

Coco leaned back in the soft leather seat and watched as Los Angeles came into view through her window. The Hollywood Hills glittered in the distance. Coco held her breath until she felt the wheels of the plane touch down on solid California ground.

As soon as the plane landed, Coco exhaled. And then she texted Mac:

I'M BAAACK!

She grinned when she saw Mac's reply.

'BOUT TIME! DRESS TO IMPRESS TONIGHT—SEE YOU AT T'S, MON AMIE. XO

Coco emerged outside baggage carousel number three, her honey-colored Louis Vuitton carry-on perched atop her L.V.-monogrammed rolling suitcase. Her mind was racing faster than a London dance remix as she scanned the crowd for Pablo, the Kingsleys' Brazilian, Swiss-trained butler. Besides the usual commotion of too many travelers waiting for too-slow-moving bags, there were at least two dozen photographers with flashes bursting like fireworks. Coco's eyes landed on a super-skinny woman with oversized D&G sunglasses and a less-than-natural platinum blond bob. She wore a cheetah-print dress and silver heels that zigzagged around her racehorse ankles.

Coco couldn't help but cringe. *Mom.*

Cardammon almost never went to the airport—or anywhere in public, for that matter—because everywhere she went she created a frenzy. The paparazzi trailed her to Whole Foods. To Coffee Bean. To Rodeo

Drive. Even now, a decade after her heyday, Cardammon still inspired global curiosity.

Cardammon took a few dainty steps toward the photographers, her face tilted slightly to the left—her good side. As a rule, Cardammon did not show teeth in pictures. Smiling was *sweet* and *wholesome*, and Cardammon was *sexy* and *edgy*.

Spotting Coco, Cardammon gave her signature wave, a few flicks of three fingers, like she was slipping on invisible rings. Before the cameras had a chance to snap Coco's picture, Cardammon's two Bosnian bodyguards, Radko and Smail, cleared a path to the black Escalade idling curbside.

"Luvvy, I've missed you," Cardammon said, squeezing Coco's cheeks when they were tucked inside the black leather backseat of the Escalade. Coco leaned back and breathed in the familiar smell of her mother's perfume as the car pulled away from the terminal and headed toward Bel-Air. "Aaaaand do you know who else has missed you?" Cardammon unzipped her oversize silver Balenciaga duffel.

"Madonna!" Coco said, kissing her French bulldog's adorably squished face.

A few photographers jogged alongside the vehicle, trying to get any last shots of her mother.

"When will they get tired of this?" Cardammon

asked, pouring herself some San Pellegrino from the mini fridge. It was more an observation than a question. Coco's mom brushed off paparazzi the way other mothers brushed lint from cheap cashmere.

"So, luvvy." Cardammon squeezed a lemon wedge into her water with her glittery purple fingernails. "Tell me everything." She crossed her legs at the ankles and gazed into Coco's dark, almond-shaped eyes.

"Mom, I got soooo much better," Coco said in one breath. "My dancing is like up here," she said, touching the roof. She had waited for this moment all summer, to finally relate to her mom, artist to artist. *And maybe soon pop star–to–pop star?*

"Did you '*absolutely sour*'?" Cardammon asked in a very deep, melodramatic voice, doing a dead-on impression of Marcel. Coco giggled. Most people had no idea her mother was so funny.

"Oh, yes, indeed." Coco volleyed back her best Marcel. Madonna snorted next to them, as if in on the joke.

"Well, that's just brill," Cardammon said, patting Coco's knee. She reached into the fridge again and pulled out a sushi bento box. "Right before I picked you up I was on the phone with Brigham."

Coco's heart paused for a beat.

Brigham.

As in Brigham Powell, as in the biggest pop producer in the world, as in make-you-or-break-you huge. He'd begun his career with Cardammon and had churned out girl groups and mega-starlets every year since then.

Coco curled her toes up in her apple-green Lanvin flats just to stay calm.

"Brigham says that *duos* are back, with a vengeance."

Coco sank a little in her seat. This wasn't what she'd been expecting to hear. She was a *singlo*, not a duo.

"Producers won't even look at you unless there are two of you," Cardammon continued, reaching for a piece of pickled ginger with her chopsticks. "And so," she said with a professionally enhanced smile, "I found you a partner. Someone huge," she added, waving her chopsticks for emphasis.

"Who is it?" Coco's mind raced imagining "huge" people her mother knew well enough to call. Vanessa Hudgens? Ashley Tisdale? Someone better?

"You'll find out at rehearsal tomorrow," Cardammon said mysteriously. "You're going to love her. Just trust me, she's *wicked*."

Coco cringed at her mother's British slang, which

didn't always translate so *brill* into American English. Why wasn't her mom telling her yet? Maybe her mom was afraid she'd get intimidated? What if this new person was *too good* and Coco dragged her down?

"After all, *some* girl has to be a new pop star this year," she said breezily, as though becoming a megastar were just another after-school job, like working at Cold Stone Creamery or the Gap. "So why not you?"

Coco shrugged. This was a valid point. Why *not* her?

CHAPTER FIVE

Emily & Paige's L.A. Itinerary

Tuesday, September 1

7 PM   Watch TV until we fall asleep

9:30 PM   Or not . . . (!!!)

Emily and Paige had expected velvet ropes (check) and paparazzi (check) and red carpets (check again) in front of the *Sea Devils* premiere party, but they had forgotten to expect a doorman with a clipboard holding a list of names.

A list that definitely did not include *their* names.

The red carpet was set up on Hollywood Boulevard, outside the main entrance to the Roosevelt Hotel. After walking around the block and finding no other way to enter the building, Paige and Emily were standing off to the side, staring at the man with the list like they were brides in the Monique Lhuillier showroom—he had something they really, *really* wanted.

"You know what? I'm an actress," Paige said finally, as though the answer had been right under her nose the whole time. Emily was about to point out that acting like Rizzo—she'd played the role in their school's production of *Grease* last year—probably wasn't going to help them get into a chichi Hollywood premiere party, but bit her tongue. "I'll get us in." Paige took a deep breath and marched confidently up to the big man in front of Teddy's while Emily watched from behind a cardboard cutout of Davey in a wet suit, the words *Sea Devil* adorning his chest.

"Name?" he asked, without glancing at Paige. He had a shaved head and wore a black suit and an even blacker shirt and tie, like some kind of Russian mobster.

Paige opened her A&W Root Beer Lip Smackers–glossed pout, but no sound came out.

"Name?" List Guy said again, this time looking down at Paige.

"My name . . ." Paige paused, as though she'd been asked a very difficult question.

Please inhale. Emily wanted to shake her friend out of her nerves. Moments like these made Emily a little sad that her friend wanted so desperately to be an actress, because the whole *performing* element really wasn't her strong suit.

List Guy took a long, exasperated breath. "I can't let you in if you're not on my list." He unclicked the velvet rope to admit two Paris Hilton look-alikes in open-backed dresses.

"I'm Davey Woodward," Paige said finally.

Emily gasped.

"And I'm Avril Lavigne," he shot back.

"Wait, let's back up." Paige reached her hands out as if to stop time. "I meant I'm *here* to *see* Davey Woodward. I'm Paige Harrington. I'm sure there's been a big mistake."

"I'm not too worried about that, *Paige*. Again, you're not on my list." He waved to the street with his clipboard. "Go home before your parents call the police."

"But you don't understand!" Paige whined loud enough for everyone in line behind her to hear. A few paparazzi near Emily shifted impatiently, waiting for the real celebrities. Without another word, Paige turned around and walked shamefacedly back to the cardboard cutout of Davey.

Emily hated to see her friend look so bummed. They were surrounded by Hollywood—*real* Hollywood, the Hollywood they read about and watched on TV. The Hollywood they'd come to Los Angeles to see.

A limo pulled up in front of them and a blond girl about their age climbed out with her family. "Maybe

I can give it a shot? It's always easier to go second," Emily offered.

Paige sighed. "It's completely useless, but why not?"

Emily took a deep breath, put one checkerboard Van in front of the other, and started to walk.

It was a balmy California night, and Emily was wearing a tank top Paige had embroidered with tiny silver beads and her favorite thrift-store-cool Levi's miniskirt. The Vans had been a last-minute addition to help her tiptoe out of the hotel room. In the few steps of her walk toward List Guy, Emily realized that she had absolutely no clue what she was going to say when she got there. And then it came to her:

"Pah-don me, sir?" Emily said, in a demure Southern accent. "May I puh-lease be let into the party?"

"Name?" he barked.

"Corey Woodward," Emily replied instantly. She knew from watching *The Davey Woodward E! True Hollywood Story* at least twenty-three times that he had a cousin, Corey, from Nashville, Tennessee. Not only that, Corey was about Emily's age and had an accent so strong it almost sounded fake.

List Guy's head popped up on "Woodward" and he squinted his dark eyes at Emily. But he didn't point at the street, and he actually looked at the list, which made her think she still had a shot. "Well, *Corey*, any reason why you're not on my list?"

Emily knew she had to stay sweet. She smiled like they'd been friends for years. "There's every reason in the *w-o-r-l-d*, sir. I originally told Davey I couldn't come to his party because I had a cheerleadin' competition," she said in her best drawl. "And he was de-vah-stated," she added, stretching eh-ve-ry syllable, and using a breathiness she'd learned from watching *Steel Magnolias* a hundred times with her mom. For days after watching the movie she'd always say, "I do declare," in her best drawl, apropos of nothing. She'd never thought it would come in handy.

"Hmmm . . ." List Guy said, considering her story. "So why aren't you at the competition?"

"My, oh, my, you are quite the thorough *investigatah*," Emily said, playfully swatting his arm. *You're a cheerleader from the South,* she told herself, *and you are* confident. "I spah-rained my ankle and couldn't compete," Emily invented, shifting her weight onto her left leg to make it seem like she was favoring it. "Which is why I'm wearin' these ahful shoes! And so I decided to surprise Davey, which is why I am not on your list, sir." Emily finished with her brightest, most pleading smile. She was starting to believe she *was* from The South. Even her sprained ankle hurt a little.

"Girlie, I want to believe you—"

"I'm sure you hear a lot of stories." Emily nodded sympathetically. "Let me show you my ID," she said, rifling through the faux Gucci she'd bought on Hollywood Boulevard for fifteen dollars. "Oh no!" She screwed up her face and made a surprised, distraught face, imagining being given a pop algebra quiz. "This is a new bag, see, and when I switched purses I must not have put my wallet in." She sighed dramatically.

List Guy took a deep breath. Emily sensed she was *thisclose*. He looked down at his clipboard. "Why don't you call your cousin on his cell?"

Emily looked up with her big brown eyes. She let her naturally curly eyelashes flutter a couple times. "I'm afraid my phone is in my other bag too."

"Sorry, sweetie, there's nothing I can do." He shrugged and puffed out his chest. The buttons threatened to pop.

"It's just frustratin', because my momma let me come all this way to surprise Davey and the rest of our family," Emily said, her big brown eyes welling.

It was a skill she'd mastered when she was just

six years old—she could make herself cry on command. All she had to do was think about sad scenes from her favorite movies: Rose letting go of Jack in *Titanic*. The ending of *The Notebook*. It came in handy whenever her mom discovered she'd been playing celebrity clothing swap with Paige (i.e., cutting Johnny Depp's head out and pasting it onto Nicole Richie's body) instead of doing her earth science homework. A lone tear trickled down her cheek.

Emily made sure not to turn around until the teardrop slid off her cheek. She wanted List Guy to see the hurt he'd caused. He deserved it for Davey-blocking her. And with that, she took two limping steps back toward Paige.

"Corey!"

She turned. The list guy was looking right at her. "Okay, you're in," he told her. "But you better be who you say you are."

Emily's right leg started to tremble. It was one of the things that happened when she was really, really nervous. She swiveled around. Cameras were flashing and there was a buildup on the red carpet behind her, tanned skin and designer clothing as far as the eye could see. Finally she spotted Paige, watching from the sidewalk down Hollywood Boulevard. She ducked behind the Davey cutout.

"I can't—" Emily started to say, *go in without my friend.*

But then she heard someone yell, "Go!"

Emily turned. Paige's head popped up from Davey's wet suit–clad shoulder, like a two-headed monster. "Go!" she mouthed.

Emily smiled, her leg shaking as List Guy unclicked the velvet rope and ushered *Corey Woodward* inside.

CHapter SIX

mac

◀ Tuesday   September 1 ▶

9:30 PM Arrive at premiere

9:31 PM Check if anyone looks better than me
(take pic for future ref!)

9:32 PM Reunion with IC!

11 PM Curfew (sleepover at Becks's)

"Okay, you're in. But you better be who you say you are."

Mac watched in shock, her M·A·C mascaraed eyes wide, as the bouncer let "Corey Woodward" in ahead of her and her family.

Mac had *met* Davey's entire extended family at his housewarming party when they had all moved from their tiny Tennessee town into his thirteen-bedroom Beverly Park mansion. The real Corey Woodward was a chunky brunette with crooked teeth and a preference for bad fake tans, even now that she lived in the world capital of the *good* fake tan. This girl had silky cinnamon hair; perfectly white, almost too-bright teeth; and glowing, naturally pale skin.

Not only was this a fake Corey, she was carrying a fake bag. Mac had bought the same one for $1,295 at Fred Segal its first day on sale last year.

The knockoff's colors were right, the interlocking G's were good, and the seams all matched, but the buckles on this girl's bag were silver, and Mac knew for a fact they were supposed to be white gold.

Mac stared at the girl, impressed. Gate-crashing was one thing. Carrying a faux Gucci to an A-list premiere party was another. And pretending to be the relative of a major movie star was in a league of its own. That took courage. She almost wanted to congratulate the girl on getting into the party.

Except not. Mac was in no mood to be that generous, when here she was, a member (albeit not pictured) of Hollywood's über-family, standing behind the velvet rope while a nobody walked past. Her mom had stopped to introduce Jenner to LeShon Williams, the highest-scoring center in the NBA and an Initiative client, but now it looked like they were actually *waiting*. Armstrongs didn't *wait*.

Not only that, her BFFs, whom she had *not seen in 83 and 65 days*, respectively, were inside that party. And they would be *waiting* for her. It was a sign of disrespect to make people wait, and Mac did not believe in disrespecting the I.C.

"Mom, let's go in." Mac tugged on the sleeve of her mom's charcoal Miu Miu sweaterdress.

Mac watched as the girl with the fake Gucci trotted

through the hotel lobby up ahead of them and into the party. She was faking it almost as flawlessly as her near-perfect knockoff bag.

Inside the Roosevelt, Teddy's had been redesigned to match the *Sea Devils* underwater/deep-sea-fishing/hell-unleashed theme. There were gigantic aquariums with koi swimming at eye level, and cocktail waitresses dressed as mermaids walked around with trays of sushi. Mac shuddered at the cannibalistic implications and made her way through the bar and out to the poolside area of the Roosevelt.

Then she paused and glanced around. It was a calculated pause, as much about taking in the scene as it was about being seen.

Mac was wearing her second-choice outfit, a black Vince minidress with gold gladiator sandals. She looked cute, classy, and original—all without looking like she'd tried for any of those things, of course. She'd come to believe it was fate that made her change earlier. It was *destiny*! It was also known as Mom.

Mac spotted Becks and Coco sipping from bright blue martini glasses, standing underneath a lush palm tree by the pool. Coco was wearing a belted pin-striped shirtdress that looked decidedly British. Becks had worn the Marni dress and Jimmy Choos as instructed. Mac slinked over to them, hoping to surprise her friends.

"Mac!" Coco squealed when she was only a few yards away. Becks sprang to life as well, tossing her sushi aside. The three girls were a tangle of tan arms and I-love-you's, accompanied by lots of unintelligible squealing.

The Inner Circle was together again.

When Mac stepped out of the hug, she double-checked her BFFs. And when she sized up Becks for the second time, she gasped.

"What is it?" Becks asked, lifting her arms to reexamine her tan. "I wore SPF 45," she added defensively.

"It's not that." Mac brushed her hand through the air dismissively. "You forgot to mention that you grew like two inches. Hello Miss I-Have-Legs-That-Go-On-Forever-and-Ever."

"I grew?" Becks looked down at her impossibly long legs.

"It's just that now I can't stand in the middle when we take pictures!" Mac said with a fake pout. "But there's nothing you can do about it tonight. And at least you're wearing those adorable flats."

Coco giggled.

With that, Mac swiveled to face the rest of the

party and puckered her lips in a well-practiced smirk. The girls each stood in The Stance: one foot in front, one hip jutting out, sizing up the guests. On the other side of the pool, Cameron Diaz was talking to Drew Barrymore. The real Paris Hilton was ignoring her look-alikes. A tiny girl with long blond hair down to the middle of her back shook Orlando Bloom's hand. Probably an actress. Actresses were always on the wrong side of too thin, because the camera really did add a size.

"Who is that?" Mac asked Becks and Coco.

The girl's profile was turned toward Mac, and Mac could see her perfect little ski-jump nose. French words floated over in Mac's direction. *Bisous. Tu sais. Allucinant.* Mac had spent enough time in Paris to know that this girl had an accent. An *American* accent.

"Oh man, I think you know who that is," Becks said, sucking air through her straight teeth.

"She's, like, half her body weight," Coco added, almost spilling her turquoise virgin Blue Devil martini. It sloshed around in her martini glass.

Mac looked over at the girl again and gasped. "Maxi-Me?" she wailed her nickname for Ruby Goldman, who was in their grade at BAMS and always copied Mac's outfits, just six sizes bigger.

Tonight Ruby was wearing a dress that looked

a lot like Mac's Vince mini, but was emerald green and clearly Vanessa Bruno, a brand that was almost impossible to find outside Paris. She wore black peep-toe heels, striking the perfect, elusive, sexy/classy balance. A long filigreed gold chain hung from her neck, glinting under the blue lights.

Ruby stood in the center of a group of BAMS girls, smiling for an *L.A. Confidential* photographer. Haylie Fowler, the BAMS dance team alternate and the only chubby girl at BAMS now that Ruby was in the single-digit sizes, held Ruby's clutch, assistant style. Ellie Parker, who supposedly had a lot of experience with boys, stood on Ruby's left, leaning into her shoulder as though they'd been BFFs forever. Kimmie Tachman, the biggest gossip in school, was posed in the back. They were actually a good-looking group. They were a *force*.

"How is *she* getting photographed for anything?" Mac wondered, instantly regretting that she'd made Ruby worthy of her attention.

"Her dad hired Lindsy Smith-Zelman to do her PR," Coco said. Lindsy Smith-Zelman was L.A.'s most in-demand publicist, the person stars turned to after they checked into rehab or got caught doing something really embarrassing on TMZ. Cardammon was one of her clients.

Mac realized she was staring at Ruby—thereby making her seem interesting and thereby giving her even more power—so she stopped and pretended to look for a sushi waitress. But it was too late. Ruby was prancing toward her, her Sugar Daddy toenails poking out at Mac from her peep-toes. Kimmie, Ellie, and Haylie followed, stepping in synch. Like they'd practiced prancing together. *Had they?*

"IMac!" Ruby said sweetly, dropping a nickname for Mac as though they'd been BFFs forever. "I'm sorry I didn't call you. *Désolée*," she added, which was even worse than the nickname because it made it seem as though Mac would ever wait for a phone call from Ruby.

Mac pursed her lips. "Hey, Ruby," she said finally, forcing a wide smile.

"I'm sure you know Kimmie," Ruby said, gesturing to Kimmie Tachman, a.k.a. the Tawker. "And I'm sure you know Kimmie's dad is producing Davey's next movie," Ruby added smugly. Kimmie smiled as though she herself had accomplished something.

Actually, Mac *had* known that. Elliot Tachman produced every Hollywood blockbuster—including two of her dad's scripts.

"Where's Beth?" Coco asked Ruby, looking behind

her and around the pool area as if expecting to see Beth Cooper floating in the pool, along with the hundreds of twinkling votive lights. In seventh grade Beth had been Ruby's best—and *only*—friend.

"Someone's dad had a little too much fun day trading, if you know what I mean," Kimmie whispered conspiratorially, rubbing her fingers together to make the sign for money. "Someone's family had to move in with their grandparents in Las Vegas."

Mac raised her eyebrows. Kimmie knew—and *told*—everything.

"Ruby, wow, what happened to you?" Becks said suddenly, as if noticing Ruby's new shape for the first time.

Ruby smiled very slowly. "Do I look different?" she asked, in a brand-new baby-talk voice. Had her voice gotten a makeover too?

"Be serious, Ruby," Mac said impatiently. "What *happened* to you?"

Coco and Becks gasped a little behind Mac.

"I just learned to wear my makeup differently," Ruby told her, ignoring the obvious fact that she was no longer a whale.

"Ruby. There is no makeup that makes you lose fifty pounds," Mac said with annoyance. She looked around, hoping to spot an excuse to get away.

On the opposite side of the pool, her mom was seated on one of the oversize white deck chairs with little Maude squeezed in next to her. Kate Hudson sat in the next chair over with her son, Ryder. Mac wasn't about to bow out of this conversation to join the gymboree.

"I guess I was so busy walking all over Paris this summer that I forgot to eat," Ruby said fake-nonchalantly. Mac's gaze snapped back to Ruby. Ruby had been to Paris? Everyone knew Paris was *Mac's* place.

"I just ate like a French girl," Ruby went on, shrugging her skinny shoulders. "You know what they say—French women don't get fat."

"They don't *say* that. It's a best-selling book," Mac corrected her. "You probably don't have much time for books, though, since you're so busy with your new *friends*." Mac dropped the word *friends* coolly, as if it was an allegation. But really, who did Ruby think she was, assembling the second-prettiest and most powerful girls from BAMS and pretending they were BFFs? If there was anything Mac hated more than user-y fake friendship, it was the niggling idea that Ruby was up to something.

Ruby's eyes narrowed at Mac angrily. Behind her Kimmie and Ellie exchanged a look. Haylie cleared her throat. This was their first fight as a new group, and clearly they weren't sure how to handle it.

"I may not have time for books," Ruby said serenely, flipping her blond hair. "But I did make time for *this*." She held out her hand toward Haylie, who pulled a copy of *People* magazine out of her Cynthia Rowley hobo and dropped it into Ruby's open palm.

Mac almost gasped.

"I just *loved* reading all about you," Ruby continued, flipping through the glossy pages with her Adore-A-Ball–painted nails. "And by all about you, I mean reading that you go to middle school," she sneered. "Everyone in your family is *sooooooo* talented. And then there's you."

For a brief moment Mac wished she could dive into the glittering pool and forget all about Ruby Goldman and her own talentless existence. "Whatever," Mac said, instantly hating herself for not having a better comeback than *whatever*. "You have no idea what you're talking about. I have plenty of talent—starting with the style you've been stealing for years." She put her hands on her slim hips for emphasis, her pink fingernails digging into the soft fabric of her black minidress.

"Sure you do," Ruby cooed, the way you would cheer on a baby taking her first steps.

"Whatever," Becks seconded. With her added height she now towered over Ruby. "Everyone knows Mac's going to be social chair."

"Did I forget to mention? *I'll* be running for social chair as well." Ruby gave them her best fake smile, and her newly formed girl posse grinned in unison behind her. They looked like a pack of fashionable hyenas celebrating their kill.

Suddenly the sounds of "Sympathy for the Devil" by the Rolling Stones faded away. A mermaid-outfitted waitress breezed past with an enormous tray of fresh oysters, almost knocking Mac over. She opened her mouth to speak but felt like she really was underwater now, not just imagining it.

"Um . . ." Coco started, clearly sensing that Mac was too shocked to speak or breathe. "Why would anyone ever pick you?" Coco and Ruby had always been rivals in dance, battling it out on BAMS' semi-professional dance team, so Ruby's new I-rule-the-world campaign must have been killing Coco, too. Mac smiled at her friend gratefully.

Ruby coolly took Coco in. "Actually, I have a little surprise for when school starts." Ruby flicked her eyes back to Mac. "And by *little* I mean it's major news that is going to rock the eighth grade and make me unbeatable."

"Well, I guess that makes two of us." Mac narrowed her eyes and folded her arms. Before she fully knew what she was saying, Mac added, "I've also got major news." The second the words escaped, Mac wished she could take them back.

"Yeah, right," Ruby said, smiling coyly. "I think we all know that you've never done anything remotely special." She waved the *People* in her hand for emphasis. "Shopping at Fred Segal doesn't really count."

"That's what you think," Mac said defensively. The Inner Circle would back her up if they knew what to say, but no one knew where Mac was going with this.

Least of all Mac. She needed big news. An insta-talent.

Her eyes scanned the party, and the room went into slow-motion. She saw Jenner bumping fists with Stephen Colletti. Her dad laughing with an assistant from his last movie. Her mom talking to Davey Woodward.

"Um, any minute now," Ruby prodded. "We're *waaaay*-ting."

Across the room, a waitress in a mermaid costume held a tray in front of the fake-Corey girl who'd acted her way into the party. Mac focused on the girl, zooming in on her face like a movie close-up in slow motion. She was laughing as she took way too many pieces of sushi, her white teeth glinting. Her eyes were bright and she looked like she was having the time of her life.

Aha moment!

"I'm a talent agent," Mac said, her world zooming back to normal. She'd dropped the A-bomb before she could stop herself. "I'm representing that girl." The sentences kept spilling from her mouth like word-barf.

Becks and Coco exchanged a quick look. Mac saw their wariness and she felt it in the pit of her stomach. In her haste to find a comeback for Ruby, she'd violated one of her mother's—and her own—cardinal rules: Never show your cards until you know what your opponent is holding. Why hadn't she just said her news was a surprise, and that they'd find out on the first day of school, too?

But it was too late. There had been witnesses, including Tachman the Tawker.

Ruby snorted. Ellie and Haylie, taking their cue from Ruby, snorted as well.

"Um, Big Mac?" Ruby said, "Reality check? There's no way you're an agent. And there's no way a girl with that outfit is a working actress," she added, flipping her long blond hair. She held out her hand and Haylie placed a martini glass full of the party's signature virgin Blue Devil drink in it. "What movie did you say she was going to be in?" Ruby asked, sipping her drink daintily, her pinky finger raised.

"Actually . . ." Mac said, squaring her shoulders. It was too late to turn back now. "By the time school starts, she'll be starring opposite Davey Woodward in *Deal with It*."

Mac high-fived Becks, who was always up to celebrate even when she didn't know the reason, and smiled at Coco, who looked more than a little nervous.

"So deal with that. Boom!" Mac flashed her hands abracadabra style at Ruby, then folded her arms smugly.

Ruby's eyes flashed, a sign that her temper was about to pop like an overshaken Diet Coke. Mac smiled. She knew Ruby's problem spot: her stormy temper, which apparently could not be dieted or walked or *oui, oui*'d away.

"There's *no way* that girl is starring in a studio picture and you know it!"

"Um, Ruby, did you forget to read *French Women Don't Freak Out?*" Mac asked. Becks and Coco laughed.

As long as Ruby kept exploding, Mac kept winning. Ruby knew this, too, which was why she took a deep breath and closed her eyes, yoga style. It was always the high-strung type-A people who loved yoga.

"Fine," Ruby said with renewed calm. "Oh, and I almost forgot to give you this." She reached her hand out and gave Mac a tiny pin that said I ♥ RUBY FOR SOCIAL CHAIR. Mac took it instinctively, the needle almost piercing her hand. "In case you forget who to vote for." Ruby smiled.

"Here's nothing," Mac said, narrowing her blue eyes, her fingers closing over the pin's cold metal. "In case you forget how much I respect you."

"Game on," Ruby said simply, and turned on her peep-toe. She slinked off to the dance floor with her minions trailing behind.

As Ruby stalked off, Mac scanned the party for "Corey." Her entire life depended on this girl. And they hadn't even met.

SEVEN

Emily & Paige's L.A. Itinerary

Tuesday, September 1

10 PM   Meet Davey Woodward

10:01 PM   Fall in love
(CSP: Very, very good)

mily popped her sixth piece of eel sushi, a.k.a. *unagi*, as she'd just been informed, into her mouth. Not bad. *Not bad at all.* She surveyed the poolside area at the Roosevelt Hotel. *This* was the L.A. she had imagined, she thought, counting three men in velvet suits, two women with obvious nose jobs, and seven stars she knew by first, last, and middle names. And standing behind a cadre of bodyguards in a roped-off VIP section was Davey. *Davey Farris Woodward.* She took mental notes so that she could tell Paige everything.

Just when Emily had stuffed a way-too-big-for-one-bite piece of sushi in her mouth, a girl with ridiculously long blond hair barreled over and hugged her as though they were long-lost friends.

"Just play along," the girl whispered in her ear.

Emily couldn't say anything anyway, because she still had the monstrous wad of fish and rice in her mouth.

"That was quite a performance you pulled out on the red carpet, *Corey*," the girl said, pulling back from the embrace. "Especially since Corey Woodward is standing over there, eating a Rocky Road brownie." She pointed to a chunky brunette in a gypsy skirt standing by a dessert table, all alone. It was indeed the real Corey. She looked exactly as she had in *True Hollywood Story*, except pudgier and with a streakier fake tan.

Emily tucked her brown hair behind her ears, swallowing hard. If she was about to get kicked out of her first A-list premiere party, she wanted to stay composed. *Please let me leave quietly,* she thought to herself. *Please don't make a scene.*

"Don't worry, she must have come with Davey and not given her name at the door. Nobody else knows," the girl explained, seeing the horrified look on Emily's face.

"In fact . . ." She put her hands on Emily's shoulders. She had a smattering of pale freckles on the bridge of her nose. Emily had always hated her own freckles, but they looked pretty on this stranger. "I was so inspired that I've decided to make you a star. How would you like to work opposite Davey Woodward in his next movie?"

A star? Emily almost laughed. That seemed like the kind of thing greasy men said in TV dramas, not something people actually uttered in real life.

"You know Davey Woodward?" Emily asked cautiously. If the girl was crazy, she didn't want to say anything that might make her snap. And if she wasn't, well . . . this could be interesting.

"I'm Mackenzie Little-Armstrong. Call me Mac," the girl said. She took her hands off Emily's shoulders and rested them on her hips. She was wearing a sleek black Vince dress that Emily had seen Jessica Alba wearing in the Who Wore It Best section of *Us Weekly*. Except Mac wore it better. "I'm that woman's daughter." Mac pointed across the room to a woman in a charcoal sweaterdress talking to Davey in the VIP area. "That's my mom, Adrienne Little-Armstrong. A.k.a. Davey's agent," Mac added.

Emily actually *did* know who Adrienne Little-Armstrong was. She was always featured in those women-in-power specials in magazines and on TV.

Mac yelled, "Hi, Mom!" and waved. Adrienne waved back and gave her a what-do-you-want look.

"So what do you think?" Mac confidently fluffed

her blond mane, a set of chunky wooden bangles clanking against one another on her tan arm.

Emily glanced over her shoulder at Davey, who was hidden behind a beefy bodyguard. She could see his right arm—she'd know his elbow anywhere—next to Mac's mom. "I was actually hoping to meet Davey *tonight*," she sputtered. "Do you think—"

"Not tonight," Mac interrupted. "You don't want to meet him as a fan. You want to meet him as an equal."

"But I—" Emily began, but Mac cut her off again.

"Listen, where are you staying? We can drive you, and we'll talk more in the car. I texted my friends and they're already meeting me there."

"I'm staying in a hotel, I'm not from L.A."

"Duh." Mac smiled. "*Allons-y.*"

Before Emily could question what that French sounding word even meant, or ask how Mac knew she wasn't from L.A., or find out if she'd ever have the chance to meet Davey again, she was following the girl's blond head outside and into a Toyota Prius. Which, actually, made her less nervous than anything else about this girl. It didn't look that much different from her mom's Toyota Camry.

Mac hopped into the front seat while Emily crawled into the back. Two pretty girls were already crammed in: One was tall and tan with short reddish hair and enormous blue eyes the color of the Pacific. The other was short and petite with almond-shaped brown eyes and thick, black eyelashes.

Mac turned around to face the trio in the back seat. She waved her slim wrist to the left, her wooden bracelets jangling again. "This is Coco." She pointed to the girl with shiny dark brown hair who smelled like Miss Dior perfume. Emily gulped. Of course she knew Coco. Well, she didn't *know her* know her, but she recognized her name from, like, every celebrity TV show and magazine ever. She was Cardammon's daughter. Which meant that Emily was *one degree away from Cardammon*. She resisted the urge to tell Coco that Cardammon's first hit, "On Fire for You," was her all-time favorite song.

"Nice to meet you," Emily said, feigning obliviousness. If there was one thing she had learned from *Us Weekly*, it was that even the children of celebrities were celebrities. (Please see: Rumer Willis.) And all celebrities wanted to be treated like regular people, except with free designer clothes.

"And this is Becks," Mac said, waving her other set of wooden bangles at the girl sitting in the middle. She looked like an Abercrombie model.

"Hi, I'm Emily." She smiled.

"And that's GPS," Mac explained, pointing to a twentysomething girl wearing black cat-eye glasses behind the wheel. "She drives us everywhere."

"Hello," the girl said, turning around. "I'm Erin, Mac's mom's personal assistant. But I'm also a singer-songwriter. Whew. That was a lot of titles to just throw at you!"

Erin had brown hair in a pageboy haircut, very pale skin, and bright red lipstick. If you *really* looked at her, she was pretty, but mostly she looked like someone who spent too much time in used bookstores. Erin slipped a CD into the player and the car immediately filled with the airy sound of flute music.

Mac leaned over to whisper to the backseat. "I'm so sorry about this," she said, gesturing to the source of the pied piper tunes. "She's desperate to get my mom to come to one of her concerts. She thinks her music is going to change the world." Mac rolled her eyes and straightened in her seat again.

"Now, where are you staying?" Mac asked in a louder voice. Apparently introductions were over.

"The Econo Lodge. I think it's on Vine," Emily answered as the car pulled into traffic.

"You got that, GPS?" Mac asked. Erin nodded but didn't say anything. "Okay, so back to business. You like Davey Woodward, yes?"

67

Emily didn't want to say she more than liked him, she was *ahb-sessed*. So she just shrugged and said, "Yeah, I watch *Just the Five of Us*."

"Well, there's more to Davey than *JTFOU* and *Sea Devils*. He's making a new movie called *Deal with It*. It's about a girl who pretends to be a boy so she can get a scholarship to a boarding school. She rooms with a hot computer nerd—Davey—and they fall in love and yada yada yada." Mac made a hand motion of someone yapping, her wooden bangles banging together. "Problem is, they can't find this girl in Hollywood. Enter you."

Emily looked around the car and saw Coco and Becks smiling at her. All of a sudden she had a scary thought. She searched the Prius for hidden cameras. The show would be called *Stupid Girls from the Midwest*. "Am I on a prank show?"

"Dude, don't freak out on us," Mac said. "This is very, very real." She clasped her hands in her lap, as if to convey the seriousness of this situation.

Emily's head was spinning. Meet Davey Woodward? And be a movie star? "Why me?" she asked.

"I'm an agent," Mac said. Erin hummed along to the flute music, steering the Prius around a corner. "I know talent when I see it. And you've got *It*."

"But I've never even acted," Emily blurted.

"How do you think you got into that party tonight?" Mac asked, raising a blond eyebrow. "It's easier to get into the White House than to pull off your little stunt."

Emily smiled shyly. It had never even occurred to her that she was acting. She'd just wanted to see Davey. And then she felt a shiver of guilty pride, remembering that she had done what Paige hadn't been able to do.

"I mean, even if I can't make you a star—*which I can*," Mac emphasized, "it could be a fun way to meet Davey." She finished nonchalantly. The word *Davey* pinged inside Emily like a bell. Emily wanted to believe her, but the girl was probably twelve. *Maybe* thirteen.

"Do you have a card?" Emily said finally. It seemed like a smart, business-y thing to ask.

"They're being printed," Mac answered smoothly. She wrote her cell phone number on a cardboard coaster from the party. Davey's face was printed on it, smiling up at her encouragingly. "Just so you know, I don't give out my cell number to just anyone. This is kind of a big deal."

Emily nodded quietly and turned to face the window. She smiled at her own rose-cheeked reflection.

The car came to a stop and Mac looked out the

tinted window at the Econo Lodge. "Is this your hotel?" she asked, the way you'd say, *Are you okay?* to someone who'd just fallen down a staircase.

Coco and Becks followed Mac's gaze and then looked sadly at Emily. Until that moment, it hadn't occurred to Emily to be embarrassed about staying there. True, it was cheap and dinky compared to the Roosevelt Hotel, but it had clean sheets and the maid had left a bunch of magazines for them yesterday. What else did you really need on vacation?

"Well, um, thanks," Emily nodded and hopped out of the car.

Mac blew an air kiss. "Call me!" she said, making a phone sign with her fingers.

Emily stood on the sidewalk outside the Econo Lodge, holding Davey's face and this stranger's number in the palm of her hand.

"So are you Emily *Woodward*?" Paige whispered in the dark, with her retainer lisp, as Emily crawled into the Econo Lodge bed next to her.

"No. More bizarre," Emily said, pushing several pillows off the side of the bed.

"Sorry, I had to stuff it," Paige explained. "Your mom woke up to go to the bathroom. I couldn't take any chances." Emily smiled at her friend in the dark.

Just then, Lori let out her signature snore, which assured the girls she was definitely not getting up any time soon.

"Now, tell me everything!"

Emily filled Paige in on her crazy night, from the ridiculous air kisses to the offer to act with Davey Woodward.

"Wait a second," Paige hissed when Emily got to the part about Mac being her agent. "This girl wants to represent you? She's never seen you act."

"She saw me *lie*." Emily splayed her cinnamon-brown locks over the pillow and looked at the hotel room's popcorn ceiling. Outside a siren wailed.

"Well, you have to at least call her in the morning," Paige told her. The colored lights of the passing police car flashed on the bumpy ceiling. "You never know what might happen."

That was true. People got discovered all the time, but they weren't usually people like Emily Mungler from Cedartown, Iowa. The girls were quiet for a minute, listening to the traffic outside, the low hum of the air conditioner, Emily's mom's occasional sleep-snorts.

"Emily?" Paige asked quietly. Emily felt her

stomach tighten. She knew what was coming—Paige was the actress, not her. Emily was supposed to go to the party to get Davey, not get discovered.

"Yeah?" Emily whispered back.

"Welcome to Hollywood!" Paige squealed, grabbing Emily's hand under the starchy sheet and squeezing it. "You're gonna be a star!"

chapter
eIGHT

mac

◀ Tuesday   September 1 ▶

11:05 PM   Exit party, pose for photogs

11:45 PM   Post-party recap at Becks's
           BNE (cont.)!

Mac leaned back in Becks's Malibu hot tub overlooking the Pacific Ocean, her blond hair floating around her like a mermaid's. The Inner Circle was listening to the crashing waves, drinking pomegranate mocktails, and enjoying a post-party recap.

"You really think you're going to make that random girl a star?" Coco asked.

"Absolutely," Mac said, faking confidence.

"But you also said you were going to be a tango dancer," Becks reminded her. "Until you met Jacob."

Mac sank a little lower into the hot water. She couldn't tell Becks or Coco the truth: If she could prove this girl had talent, then she would have talent, too. They wouldn't understand—Becks and Coco had more talent in their freshly painted peony-pink pinky toes than Mac had in her entire body.

Besides, there was something even bigger at stake than Mac's talent-slash-lack-thereof: the future of the Inner Circle. If Ruby Goldman became social chair, she would make their lives miserable, and for the first time in their school careers, Mac, Coco, and Becks would *not* rule BAMS.

"I can make her a star," Mac said slowly, retying her American Apparel navy string bikini top. She owned seven, one in every color. Sometimes she mixed and matched the tops with the bottoms, but tonight she was totally coordinated, aka no-nonsense.

"A star on what? A reality show?" Coco teased, the ends of her chocolate-brown hair trailing in the bubbly surface of the water. "*America's Next Top Farm Girl*," she added in a breathy Tyra Banks voice.

Mac shot her a disapproving look. "A full-fledged movie star. Thanks to my big mouth, now I *have* to. If I don't, Kimmie Tachman will tell everyone, and then it's sayonara, social chair." Mac took a deep breath. "Ladies, do not forget that social chair is *the* most important position at BAMS. This person determines *all* things social. We're talking school dances, performers, lunch menus in the school cafeteria . . ."

Coco and Becks shrugged and sipped their pomegranate juices.

"If I win, that power stays with *us*," Mac said, combing her fingers through her wet hair. "But if I don't win, not only do we lose that power, it goes to *Ruby Goldman*." Mac said her name like *Ebola virus*. "You know how fun it is to be popular and be invited to all the boys' parties? Well, if we're not top tier, you can kiss all that buh-bye." She kissed her M·A·C-polished nails and fluttered her hand to illustrate.

"Why?" Coco asked, setting her clear plastic cup on the edge of the hot tub. The pomegranate juice looked bloodred in the darkness.

"Ruby will make sure we're the last to know about everything. Whatever we want won't matter. She'll turn BAMS *against* us."

"Ruby *is* mean," Coco conceded. "She fired six of her dad's seven assistants. And in fourth grade, she replaced the cotton batting in my toe shoes with oatmeal."

"When I picked her last for dodgeball she 'spilled' chocolate milk on me at lunch," Becks chimed in. "But of *course* I was going to pick her last—she was way too big a target," she added with a sly grin, bringing her arms outward in an imitation of Ruby's former girth.

"Ruby is a code-red social threat. She knows how

to throw her weight around," Mac said. "No pun intended. The girl goes after what she wants. Look at her dancing." Ruby was actually a great dancer—she and Coco would likely battle it out for BAMS dance team captaincy this year. "If she says she's got something big to announce on the first day of school, she means it," Mac said definitively, retying her bikini for the third time.

"I get it," Becks said, blinking her blue eyes. "But so what? It's just some eighth-grade position." She ran her fingertips over the surface of the water.

Moments like this reminded Mac that Becks and Coco needed her to be their ATM of social savvy. It was time to make a deposit.

"Here's the deal," Mac began, opening her hands as if she were giving a presentation at the boardroom table. "We're at a very pivotal moment in our lives. We're rising eighths, and this year is all about setting precedents. If Ruby assumes dominance now, that sets the precedent for ninth grade. Ruby will get the reputation of"—Mac made air quotes—"*the cool incoming freshman.*"

She made eye contact with Becks and Coco to be sure they were still with her. "She'll be the first freshman invited to upperclassman parties. And ninth grade sets the precedent for all of high school. So before you know what's happened, it's senior prom and Ruby Goldman is prom queen."

"We don't have a prom queen," Coco pointed out.

"That's beside the point," Mac went on, annoyed. "What I'm trying to say is that if we don't put the brakes on Ruby now, she's going to steal our spotlight, our invites, our future boyfriends—the life that is rightfully ours. All because we sat back and watched when we had a chance to stop her."

Silence. A wave crashed to the shore.

"But it doesn't end there," Mac continued, her hands forming involuntary fists under the water. "Because then you enter college *reeking* with the scarlet stamp of awkwardness. And everyone knows that 70 percent of people marry someone they meet in college and make their most important future professional connections. So basically what you're calling 'just an eighth-grade position,' Becks"— Mac eyed her friend—"is the key to the rest of our lives."

Becks dunked her head underwater as if to wash away the bad vibe.

"*Intonse*," Mac added, nodding. She loved to say random words in a French accent, and "intense" was one of them. "I just want to do the best for all of us," Mac finished, too heated to stay in the steamy Jacuzzi. She sat on the edge and dipped her toes in the water.

Coco looked at Becks, who nodded.

"We're in," Becks said determinedly. "Tell us what you need."

"Purr-fect." Mac smiled. She needed to have her girls for this one. Without them, she was just another girl with amazing hair, great clothes, and impeccable taste.

"Training for Random Girl begins tomorrow at two," Mac said, grabbing her iPhone to make the appointment official.

She piled her hair into a heavy, wet bun atop her head and sat up straighter, her posture poised and perfect. With great power comes great responsibility, and she couldn't afford to blow this one—the rest of their lives depended on it.

chapter nine

becks

8:28 AM GET UP!

8:33 AM GO SURFING!!

8:35 AM FIND AUSTIN!!!

Becks woke up to the sound of waves crashing and glanced down at her yellow G-Shock digital watch. 8:28 a.m. The Inner Circle had fallen asleep in her father's screening room, which had rows of plush velvet couches instead of movie-theater-stadium seats. (Thank you, MTV!) Their normal Saturday night ritual, or in this case Tuesday night, since it was still summer, was to watch one of Adrienne's clients' new films way before it hit theaters, scour magazines for must-have fashion items, compile a master list of said items, try out adventurous makeup techniques, paint their toenails, and then fall asleep talking and giggling under the glow of the big screen.

Becks checked to see if her friends were still asleep. Mac's mouth was hanging wide open, her arm draped lazily over her Victoria's Secret Pink pajamas.

Check. Coco was snoring every third breath, also in Victoria's Secret Pink. *Check.* Mac had a strict don't-wake-me-before-10-a.m.-on-weekends-unless-you-have-magically-become-Gwen-Stefani-or-you-are-surprising-me-with-a-trip-to-Paris policy. Her mother had done the latter the summer before fifth grade, but supposedly Mac had still been cranky all day.

Becks opened the sliding glass door that led from the screening room to the beach and picked her favorite Hawaiian flower-print surfboard out of its special rack. This was the best time to surf—the beach was empty, and the waves were killer. The morning sun was piercingly bright.

She grinned when she spotted Austin's red plaid beach blanket and his goldendoodle, Boone. As she dragged her board toward him, she felt that same fluttery light-headedness from yesterday.

"Becks, where ya been?" Austin yelled, climbing out of the surf. His body was dripping with water, and his new muscles were definitely still there. Her heart was pounding. He pulled his clingy Rusty board shorts over his tan hips and looked Becks up and down. "Is the zombie look in?"

Becks touched her face and remembered she'd fallen asleep with her smoky charcoal eye makeup still on.

She patted down her post-party hair, which was crunchy from too much product. The ends stuck out sideways, like she'd been electrocuted. "Is the wet-dog look in?" she retorted.

Austin laughed and shook his sandy-brown hair out of his eyes. "Yup. Starting with me." He reached over and tousled her already-tousled hair, dripping salty Pacific Ocean water all over her.

She shivered at the cold, or maybe at his touch. "So are we gonna surf today, or just discuss hairstyles?" Becks giggled, reaching over to muss his hair back.

"Oh, *slam!*" Austin pretended to take a sip from his water bottle but then turned the nozzle and squirted water all over Becks. She put her hands up to fake-fight but still couldn't stop giggling, not even as she ran away from him.

Becks had barely made it ten steps before Austin caught her and started giving her noogies.

"Stop!" Becks half protested. She put her hands on his shoulders, in theory to stop him, but really just because it felt good to rest them there. He looked back at her with his blue-gray eyes, and she felt her heartbeat slow down, so slow it felt like it might stop. Their faces were only inches apart and they were touching and *was he going to kiss her*?

"Becks! Hellooooo! We gotta get to brunch!" Mac's voice boomed from behind them.

Becks looked up and saw Mac and Coco, fully dressed and waiting for her on the terrace. She'd forgotten they were supposed to go eat Dutch apple pancakes at the Polo Lounge in the Beverly Hills Hotel.

She looked into Austin's eyes and slowly took her hands off his tan shoulders. "I better go," she said, faking a smile. "Ick calls."

"Catch ya later," Austin said, stepping back and giving her a casual salute. She watched him jog back toward his blanket, shaking his tousled hair out of his eyes. There was no denying it: She had a full-blown, major crush. On her neighbor. On a guy she'd always thought of as a brother.

Becks ran up the sand to catch her girlfriends, the words *I'm totally in love with Austin* on the tip of her now slightly sandy tongue. Mac and Coco were staring over her shoulder at Austin on his hands and knees, barking at Boone. She watched lovingly as he reached over and scratched his big, shaggy dog behind his ears.

"What a freak!" Mac said. It took Becks an extra second to realize Mac was talking about Austin.

"No wonder he has so much fun with his dog. He is one. Nasty."

"Ruf, ruf," Coco agreed.

"That's his new nickname. Ruf-Ruf!" Mac laughed and then high-fived Coco. Becks stared down at the beach, her sandy tongue choking her.

"I left you an outfit on your bed." Mac turned to Becks. "Lacoste sundress and sandals. Very cute. Very you." She looked Becks up and down. "You are so going to have to shower. We can't go out with you like that." She glanced at her iPhone planner and sighed. "We're gonna be late. This is not good. Not good at all."

Becks took one last look at Austin and Boone before she hurried into the house to get changed for brunch. Although her feet went one way, her heart had definitely gone another.

CHAPTER
ten

Emily & Paige's L.A. Itinerary

Wednesday, September 2

9 AM   Econo Lodge breakfast (Mini meal #1)

10 AM   Santa Monica Pier and walking tour
           (CSP: Low)

2 PM   Venice Boardwalk (CSP: Low)

7 PM   Dinner at Olive Garden
           (CSP: Impossible)

8 PM   Decide which talk show we want to attend
           taping of (CSP: Depends on whether you
           consider C-listers celebrities)

Emily took a mini box of Froot Loops, which her mother only let her eat on vacation, and poured it into the white ceramic bowl. She was still full from the sushi at the *Sea Devils* party, but her mom would definitely know something was up if she didn't jump at the chance to eat sugar cereal for breakfast.

Emily's mind was still buzzing from meeting Mac and being discovered and the thought of maybe, possibly meeting Davey. Even Los Angeles seemed sparkly: The air felt cleaner, the Econo Lodge silverware shone a little brighter, the Formica tabletop glinted in the morning sunlight.

"So, girls," Lori said, slicing a grapefruit. "I was thinking instead of Santa Monica, we could go to the La Brea Tar Pits." She smiled as if she'd just suggested a shopping spree on Robertson Boulevard, not a stroll through a desertlike park.

Emily inhaled. It was 106 degrees outside, and the thought of standing in the sun looking at cacti seemed about as fun as spending the day in the window department of Home Depot. Plus, she couldn't do that if she was going to meet up with Mac. She'd spent most of the night tossing and turning just thinking about it.

At the table next to them, a retired couple was reviewing different tour options for seeing the stars' homes. Emily had read that Lindsay Lohan had moved twice, just to keep her home off the star tour.

Emily exhaled. She was going to have to tell her mother the truth. Or at least, *some* of it.

"Mom, you know how you are always saying that we attract what we think about?" Emily began, trying to put it into terms her mother would appreciate. "Like magnets?"

"That's right," Lori said, her eyes widening, excited that someone wanted to talk self-help with her. Paige shot Emily a look.

"Well, I think about Davey Woodward a lot. And . . ." Emily inhaled. She knew that there was no turning back from what she was about to say. "LastnightImetatalentagentwhowantsmetotryoutfora-roleinDaveyWoodward'snextmovie." She rushed the words together.

Lori looked up sharply from her grapefruit, her brows knit. "What? Where?"

"Just down the, um, street from here," Emily stammered, her heart beating faster. What could she tell her mom? That she and Paige had sneaked out of the hotel and into a VIP party? "I . . . took a walk because I couldn't sleep."

Lori's eyes widened as she imagined all the horror scenarios that might have been. She blinked the vision away. "But we went to bed early."

Paige piped up. "It was my fault, Mrs. Mungler. I dragged her to a premiere party so I could meet Hollywood people, and that's when the agent discovered her. But it makes perfect sense, when you consider that all we've thought about since we landed is Davey Woodward." She looked right into Lori Mungler's eyes. "We put this out there." Paige opened her palms as though she were actually touching the universe.

Lori's gaze went from confused to stony. She set her sights on her daughter. "Emily. What were you thinking?"

"I'm so sorry, Mom," Emily said, summoning the tears that usually worked on her mother. They were half real, too.

Next to them, the couple decided on Starline Tours.

"It's the opportunity of a lifetime, Mrs. Mungler." Paige jumped in with some damage control before Lori could get more upset. "The studio has been looking everywhere for this perfect Midwestern girl, and filming has stalled until they find her."

Lori looked away for a second, and Emily knew that she was actually considering this logic. Emily gratefully squeezed Paige's hand under the table. Their friendship bracelets clacked together. "Well, maybe after you earn a college degree you can move to Los Angeles and become an actress," Lori said, waving her butter knife as she spoke.

Emily swallowed hard. She wasn't used to not being able to persuade her mother. Paige, sensing the impasse, jumped in again. "Mrs. Mungler, a lot of people have had great careers after getting discovered at places you wouldn't expect," she said matter-of-factly, removing the yolk from a hard-boiled egg. "Charlize Theron was spotted at a bank. Natalie Portman was discovered at a pizzeria."

"That's two people." Lori said, putting her knife down.

"Plus," Paige continued, "the producers are desperado with a capital *D*. The other actresses aren't available. Quinn Mallory is shooting in Italy. Anastasia Caufield will only play a boy if the script has Oscar written all over it."

The old couple at the table next to them pointed to different spots on their map thoughtfully at hearing the stars' names.

Lori looked at Paige as though she'd just pulled off her head. "How do you know all this?" she asked suspiciously.

"I have to know the industry I want to be a part of," Paige said simply. She popped the egg white into her mouth.

For the first time in the conversation, Lori smiled. "You're a funny girl, Paige."

"I know." Paige grinned back. "And as you're always telling us, when it's right, it's easy. Well, Mrs. Mungler, this could not have been more right or more easy. Trust me."

Emily almost cried real tears, hearing her friend plead so passionately to get her an opportunity Paige had dreamed of for herself.

Lori drummed her fingers on the table. She looked around the breakfast room. The swirly hotel carpet had faded in the sunlight. Outside, the rush-hour traffic was beginning to bustle. No one spoke for seconds. Finally she said, "First I want to meet this agent."

Emily opened her mouth wide as though she were going to scream, but instead she pressed her hands against her cheeks. Paige hugged her.

Emily pulled the Davey coaster from her pocket and began dialing. She wanted to hurry up and get this meeting before her mother changed her mind. She just hoped that Mac hadn't changed hers.

CHAPTER
eLeven

mac

◀ Wednesday   September 2 ▶

10 AM Wake up

11 AM Brunch/Major strategy session
       re: new star

1 PM   Discuss new client with Mom

Sitting at La Conversation peeling flaky layers off her cinnamon-almond cream brioche, Mac allowed herself thirty more seconds to be annoyed at Becks and then she was going to drop it forever. Because Becks had been busy playing with Ruf-Ruf, they'd been too late to keep their Polo Lounge reservation.

Instead, they'd been forced to go to La Conversation in West Hollywood. Which would have been fine if Mac had been looking forward to going to La Conversation. Or if she'd had her Vanessa Bruno pewter dress rush dry-cleaned to go to La Conversation. Or saved her Sigerson Morrison flats to debut at La Conversation. But no, she'd spent the morning imagining her fashion-perfect appearance at the Polo Lounge, where she was guaranteed the pleasure of seeing and being seen.

Mac sighed and decided to take in the good things about La Conversation: the French country-chic décor, the scent of baking cupcakes, and the fact that her two best friends were staring at her expectantly. She had zapped an agenda to Becks's and Coco's iPhones to remind them of things they needed to discuss at this brunch:

Topics to cover:
1. How am i going to make this random girl a movie star?
2. Social chair campaign stragegies.
3. Is my hair officially too blond? Lowlights?

"Seriously, girls, focus!" Mac said as their soy lattes were served. "The only person I know who can make nobodies into movie stars is my mother, and she's O-O-T until Saturday."

"Mama Armstrong is out of town?" Coco said, fully understanding the magic that only Adrienne Little-Armstrong could work. Her dark hair was held in place by a thin black velvet headband—a good, versatile choice, Mac noted, as it was both Polo Lounge preppy as well as Paris-schoolgirl cute.

Mac nodded solemnly. "She's visiting Tristin in New Zealand and she leaves tonight." Tristin

Andrews had won two Best Actress Oscars and was currently shooting a family drama in New Zealand that was expected to deliver Oscar number three. "So I have one shot at convincing her to help me out, and that's in, like, an hour," Mac told her best friends, shaking out her long blond hair. "I just have to hope that she'll see how serious I am about this."

The Inner Circle was sitting at a round bistro table in the center of the packed dining room. Red and white fabric cascaded down the walls from the pink glass chandeliers, and blue and white curios lined the countertop.

"Of course she's going to be on board," Coco said, always positive. "I mean, *everyone* knows how good your taste is, especially your mom."

Mac nodded. Coco had a point.

"And speaking of moms, you'll never believe what Cardammommy told me—"

Coco was cut off by Mac's phone, blaring her Pussycat Dolls "Dontcha" ringtone in the quaint French restaurant. Diners on either side of them turned to look, then returned to their meals. It was a private number. On a Wednesday morning. Mac picked up on the fifth ring. "Who are you and what do you want? I'm in a very important breakfast meeting."

The voice on the other end sounded scared. "Hey, um, Mac. It's Emily? We met last night?"

"Oh, *Emily*," Mac said sweetly. "Sorry I just gave you my phone voice. I didn't recognize the number. How *are* you?"

Emily breathed an audible sigh of relief. "I'm calling because my mom wants to meet you."

"No problem," Mac answered. "Urth Café on Melrose at three."

"Great," Emily answered. "Where is that?"

"Ask anyone." *Click.*

Mac smiled at her reflection in one of the many gold-framed mirrors covering La Conversation's walls, secretly pleased at how blasé she'd managed to sound. There was no way Mac could let this girl know how overjoyed she was that she'd called. Mac was new at managing talent, but she knew one thing for sure: It was never, ever cool to show how badly you needed someone.

"All righty," Mac said, expertly typing the new plan into her iPhone. "We've got a prelim meeting set up for today, and I'd like to get in some makeover work tomorrow. Fred Segal? We can shop for dresses for Kimmie's party and make Emily L.A.-pretty."

Becks rolled her eyes before nodding along with

Coco. Kimmie Tachman's Sweet Thirteen party was this Friday and they were all going. To Becks, lip gloss and shopping were like the chandeliers at La Conversation: fussy overkill.

"And then we can go over social chair campaign strategies at Pinkberry," Mac said, glancing at the next item on her Topics to Cover list.

"We should probably get her an invite to Kimmie's party," Coco noted. She sipped her latte through a striped straw because she was afraid to stain her teeth.

"Point for you!" Mac said to Coco. "Absolutely. We have to establish that she's one of *us* now."

"Hasn't the guest list been closed for weeks?" Becks asked.

"Becks, you need to start coming to me with *good* news," Mac groaned. She twirled her Tiffany kite scroll drop earring with her right hand. Becks was right. Kimmie's guest list was sealed shut. Everyone in town wanted to suck up to Kimmie's dad, and a killer thirteenth b-day present was the quickest way.

Mac sighed. "I'll figure it out la-tah."

She pulled up her iPhone again to make sure they'd covered all the bases. "All righty. Saturday night we'll have our regular sleepover chez Becks," Mac noted. "And if all goes well, our special screening will be our gal's audition tapes, and we'll be celebrating her new role."

She smiled as if this were all as easy as flashing an AmEx. But she knew it was going to take a lot more than a platinum card.

Mac walked into her mother's sleek office at Initiative. She felt good about her outfit: a black skirt from Lisa Kline with a Petit Bateau tee and Marc by Marc Jacobs kitten heels. Dressing the part was a Mac priority at all times, and today the part was in-control agent-in-training. She needed to convince her mom to take on one more new client.

Initiative's main office was in Beverly Hills, just a few blocks from Rodeo Drive. It looked like a futuristic airport, with wall-to-wall windows, marble floors, and aquariums filled with rare fish everywhere. All the walls were painted red, since it was the power color, and Initiative was *all* about power.

Adrienne sat behind a wall with a square cut out in the middle. When she needed privacy, she could close the panel with a remote control. Her two assistants, Charlotte and David, sat in front of her door, guarding her office like lions. Charlotte was the first assistant, and she handled communication with other offices. David was the second assistant, and his job was to make restaurant reservations, buy presents for clients, and do anything Charlotte didn't get to.

Charlotte and David looked exhausted, but they instantly perked up when they spotted Mac.

"Mac, how is the cutest girl in Beverly Hills?" Charlotte asked without waiting for an answer. Supposedly her dad was a New York billionaire, a fact not unnoticed by the partners at Initiative. "I tried on that skirt at Lisa Kline last week, but I couldn't pull it off. *Lucky ducky*," she added, fake-jealously. Mac smiled. She knew it was part of Charlotte's job description to be nice to her, but she reveled in the compliment anyway.

"Mac, great to see you," David whispered, his ear to the phone. He was listening in on one of Adrienne's calls so she would have a record of her conversation. Eavesdropping was actually part of his job. "You guys, they still haven't found a girl for *Deal with It*," he hissed to Charlotte and Mac, his eyes twinkling with the gossip. "They had 182 girls dressed as boys lined up outside the studio this morning!"

Mac nodded politely as if this news had no bearing on her, her insides doing somersaults. They still had time to get Random Girl the role.

When Adrienne finished talking on the phone, she poked her head through the square hole in the wall.

"No more calls for now," Adrienne said as she spotted her daughter. "Unless it's Davey. Everyone else, I'll return when I'm back in L.A."

Mac carefully entered her mother's office, which was technically a corner suite. It had a private bathroom, a walk-in closet, an elliptical machine, and a kitchenette. The windows faced Barneys and Wilshire Boulevard on the south side and the Hollywood Hills on the east side. Mac sank down in one of the buttery leather chairs facing her mother's clear Lucite desk.

Adrienne pushed her rectangular Armani glasses low over her nose and looked down at Mac. "What's up? Everything okay? Did Maudy take apart the espresso machine to make a computer again?"

"No, nothing like that. I'm sorry to ask a weird question . . ." Mac began.

"Don't apologize for yourself. It's a terrible habit girls have, always saying sorry." Adrienne panto-mimed zipping her lips. "But please, if there are no more apologies, go on."

"Okay." Mac ran her tongue over her newly debraced teeth. "Do you ever wonder what makes someone a movie star?" Mac asked.

"The It factor," Adrienne replied, without thinking.

"Right, but what is *It*?" Mac asked the question

that had kept her up late last night while her friends had fallen asleep in the blue light of the screening room.

"Sweetheart, if we knew, then there would be no movie stars, because everyone would have *It*." Adrienne raked sand in the Japanese rock garden on her desk. "*It* would be flying off the shelves."

Mac smiled. She was on the right track.

"Mackenzie, may I ask where we're going with this?" Adrienne asked, looking at her gold Baume & Mercier watch.

Mac sat up a little straighter, which was difficult in the soft leather of the chair. "I met a girl at the party last night. And she's got *It*. She's the next best thing. And she's going to be at Urth Café today. And I told her we'd be there at three to discuss *Deal*—"

"Wait. Stop." Adrienne interrupted, putting her hands into the time-out sign. "You know my rule. I don't represent friends."

"Mom, this is *not* a friend. This is something different," Mac insisted. She could feel her heart beating faster. Her mother wasn't even letting her finish her sentences. She had to get her on board before she left for New Zealand.

"Sweetheart, in this town, everyone and their dog knows someone who is perfect for a role. And the fact that I'm an agent is *not* going to give your friends a connection. We've discussed this time and again."

"Mom, I know I'm violating a huge family rule here, but that's how much this means to—"

"I don't have time to discuss this now," Adrienne said, glancing at her watch again. "I love you and I love that you've got ideas, but I have a call sheet with two hundred people on it. We'll discuss this all you want Saturday at brunch." Mac and her mom had a mother-daughter brunch every other Saturday at the Beverly Hills Hotel. Adrienne's e-mail alert dinged and she swiveled in her Aeron chair to face her enormous flat-screen computer monitor.

Mac's short, polished fingernails dug into her Lisa Kline skirt. For all she knew, Random Girl would be gone by Saturday. "But, Mom—"

"You know, it's not as easy as you might think to spot talent," Adrienne mused, not looking up from the e-mail she was typing. "Real actors are so good you can't even catch them acting—they just *become* someone else." She looked back at her daughter, blinking behind her rectangular glasses. "They can fool *anyone*."

Adrienne kissed her fingertips and mimed throwing a kiss at Mac, who very listlessly mimed catching it, knowing full well that the conversation was over. Then Adrienne flipped her mouthpiece back in front of her face. "Get me Spielberg," she yelled to Charlotte, fully back in agent mode.

As Mac's kitten heels clicked down the space-age hallway, she tried to stay calm. It was two thirty, she had the meeting of her life in half an hour, and there was no way Adrienne would be there.

Mac reached the door to the parking lot, where Erin was waiting in the Prius. As the motion-sensor doors closed behind her, Mac realized she wasn't just walking away from Initiative. She was walking away from the possibility that her mom was going to help her make this unknown girl a star.

Mac was going to have to tackle this one on her own.

chapter
TWELVE

COCO

◀ Wednesday   September 2 ▶

12 PM   Back to Bel-Air

1 PM   Meet mystery partner???

oco was stretching in her dance studio, on the top floor of her father's King Bel-Air Hotel. On one side of the studio were floor-to-ceiling mirrors polished by the hotel staff twice a day, and on the other side were plate-glass windows overlooking the hotel courtyard's turquoise Olympic-size pool. The door handles were interlocking back-to-back CKs, like the Calvin Klein logo but inverted. The logo was even frosted onto the glass door.

Coco had learned from Marcel Marcel to channel an animal for five to ten minutes before starting a dance workout. It was extraordinarily odd and avant-garde, but Marcel Marcel swore it tapped into creativity and unleashed inhibitions, so today Coco was a turtle. Being a turtle forced her to slow down her movements and really feel the way her joints came together. She was crawling on all fours, flicking her tongue, stretching her neck out, and squeezing it into her shoulders.

"Coco?"

Coco looked up just as her tongue was mid-flick. Her mother was standing in the double-height doorway wearing an underwear-length white tennis skirt and a tight stretchy silver top that tied behind her neck. It was part of the Cardammon line she'd designed for H&M, and definitely not appropriate mother-wear.

"Luv, your new partner is here," Cardammon said with a sly smile. She stepped to the side of the doorway.

Coco's mind raced excitedly as she imagined who might walk in. Hilary Duff? Jamie-Lynn Spears, ready to follow in her sister's pre-rehab footsteps? The cute whatshername Cheetah Girl? Before Coco could stand up and get out of her turtle position, in through the doorway walked . . .

Ruby Goldman.

"Hey, Coco," Ruby said in that baby-talk voice she'd used last night. She wore a black leotard with a Stella McCartney for Adidas jersey skirt. She put a hand on her hip, as though it were totally normal for her to be standing in Coco's private penthouse dance studio.

Still on her hands and knees on the floor, Coco stood up slowly. She could feel the apricot-jelly-and-butter crepes she'd eaten at La Conversation rise up in her throat.

Her new partner was Ruby Goldman? She looked at her mom to say *no way*. But Cardammon was looking back and forth between the two girls and beaming proudly at the duo's potential. Coco gulped.

"Luv, you and Ruby are going to be fab together," Cardammon said, flashing her bright white teeth at her daughter. "Why don't you show Ruby your dance?" Cardammon winked.

Coco brushed a piece of lint off of her stretchy black L.A.M.B. pants and nodded to her mother to press play. Her own song "Do What I Want" blared over the speakers and she performed her Marcel-approved routine, trying to "feel the music" and "soar," but it was hard to let loose with Ruby standing with her back against the dance studio's bar, surveying Coco's every move.

Ruby watched for the first few minutes, and then, as if to show that she got it, jumped in and started dancing. If Coco hadn't been reeling from the shock of seeing Ruby, she would have been impressed by how quickly Ruby nailed the dance steps, picking up the routine as though she'd been rehearsing for weeks.

Coco looked at her own reflection in the gleaming wall-to-wall mirrors. Ruby danced behind her like a shadow. A blond, skinny, perky shadow, who didn't make a mistake. Yes, Ruby was an excellent dancer. But she was *Ruby*. She was her best friend's enemy. Which meant she was Coco's enemy, too.

Instead of concentrating on her dance steps, all Coco could think was, *This will never work*. She forgot her place and stumbled over her feet. Then she collided with Ruby, sending them both tumbling onto the shiny maple dance floor.

"Sorry," Coco said, extending a hand to help Ruby up. She stole a glance at her mother, hoping her screwup would convince Cardammon this was a terrible idea.

Cardammon laughed as she stopped the music with the remote. "You've gotten your first naff moment out of the way. Now you'll be brill," Cardammon howled.

Coco tried to find the best way to gracefully bow out of this terrible situation. She didn't know how to tell her mom that she'd never work with Ruby.

"Brill!" Ruby said fakely, smiling at Cardammon. She tugged at her jersey skirt and nodded positively, her blond ponytail bobbing.

Cardammon walked to the center of the dance

floor to face the girls, her four-inch platforms clomping noisily. "I have big, big news, Coco. Are you ready?" Cardammon patted the tops of her thighs as though making a drumroll.

Coco nodded numbly. She'd had so many surprises that day, she'd maxed out her ability to feel shock. "Okay," she said a little warily.

"Clear your calendars this Saturday. You girls have an audition with Brigham."

Coco's jaw dropped.

Brigham.

On Saturday.

Ruby beamed and clapped her petal-pink manicured fingers.

Coco watched Ruby's image in the mirror. And then Coco realized: Ruby had known about this all along. *This* was the secret she was going to unveil on the first day of school. Ruby and Coco were going to be a Brigham-endorsed duo.

It was a dream come true.

And it would also win Ruby social chair.

Mac was going to kill her.

chapter THiRTeen

mac

◀ Wednesday   September 2 ▶

3 PM   First meeting with new client

4 PM   Practice with new client

11 PM   Beauty rest

The afternoon sun beat down on Mac as she made her way back through the Initiative parking lot to where Erin was waiting in the Prius. Mac slumped in the passenger seat and stared at the sunroof.

"Did you see Nicole Richie?" Erin asked.

Sometimes Mac wondered if Erin just flipped through pages of *Us Weekly* and threw out names, like darts, to make idle conversation. Nicole Richie wasn't even repped by Initiative.

Erin had been her mom's personal assistant—and by extension Mac's assistant—for two years. She had very round, very green eyes that looked extra round and extra green today. Her brown hair was piled in Princess Leia buns on the sides of her head, secured by olive-colored barrettes. She was twenty-seven but she seemed forty-seven. Or seven. Or maybe just crazy.

"Hey, Erin, I need you to make one stop at Urth Café," Mac said in her nicest voice.

"You betcha," Erin said. "Off we go!"

Mac didn't even notice that Erin was playing her freaky flute-and-harmonica music because she was too busy trying to figure out how she could possibly pull off her first and only deal as a talent agent without her mother's help. Her breath felt heavy in her chest. Every time she inhaled, she remembered there was a girl from Iowa expecting to meet Adrienne Little-Armstrong. As Erin turned up an empty La Cienega Boulevard, Mac wished for traffic to slow them down. She needed a plan. What could she possibly tell Emily's mother?

1. Adrienne was sick (lame).
2. Adrienne was in a super-urgent meeting (brush-off).
3. Adrienne broke her arm (Adrienne had broken her arm once in a skiing accident, so it wasn't a *complete* lie).
4. Adrienne left early to go to New Zealand (totally possible, but also totally not true).

Mac squeezed the door handle tighter on the Prius as they neared Urth. The fact was that Adrienne would not be there. And that would be a huge red flag to Emily's mother, who, if she was anything like Mac's mother, would whisk her daughter away to Disneyland and never look back.

Without Adrienne Little-Armstrong, Mac was just a twelve-year-old girl trying to convince some Midwestern mother she could make her daughter a movie star. Unfortunately, Mac realized, no matter how much *she* trusted herself, she couldn't expect some random stranger to do the same. She needed an adult to vouch for her, whether she liked it or not.

"Oooh, good parking karma today!" Erin exclaimed, pulling into a spot directly in front of the popular café. Erin was like the North Star of how Mac didn't want to be when she was an adult. And then Mac smiled, realizing: Erin *was* an adult.

"Erin, I have a teeny-tiny favor to ask of you," Mac said, deliberately speaking in a way that made her sound a little younger and a little sweeter.

"Sure, Mac. Anything." Erin smiled as she turned off the car and put the key in her red satchel. It had tassels and tiny mirrors embedded in the side.

"I need you to pretend to be my mom."

Erin looked around the car as though it were bugged. "That's your idea of a *teeny-tiny* favor?"

"Erin. I need your help because I'm meeting

Emily, the girl you met last night, today, and her mother is expecting to meet my mother. If I can't convince the mom that I can make her a star, I won't get to be social chair," she quickly explained, as though this made perfect sense. She twirled her Mintee bracelet for good luck.

"How could you not get social chair?" Erin said, scoffing at the injustice. She'd heard Mac talking about it for the last two years now. "You've been the cat's pajamas at BAMS forever."

Mac smiled at Erin's loyalty and decided to ignore the fact that Erin had just said *cat's pajamas*. "I know, but I told Ruby Goldman that I could get this girl a part, and now my reputation depends on it. She's gonna be big. We're talking Emma Roberts huge. You won't even have to lie; just don't correct me when I say you're my mom. Besides, she'd totally be here doing this if she weren't leaving for New Zealand today."

Erin looked straight ahead and gripped the steering wheel so tightly that her knuckles turned white. She hadn't said yes, but she hadn't said no, either.

Mac knew this was her only chance. Her mind raced, trying to think of what would persuade Erin. The flute music floated in and out of her ears. *You have to figure out what the other person wants.*

"I'll make you a deal. You pretend you're my mom and I'll deliver her to your next concert." Erin was always inviting Adrienne to come see her gigs. Of course Adrienne never went. "I don't care if it's in Silverlake or Seattle, I'll get my mom there."

Erin blinked her green eyes, just enough for Mac to know that she was on the verge of a yes.

"I don't know . . ." Erin shrugged, and her peacock-feather earrings touched her shoulders. She unbuckled her seat belt.

Mac grabbed her purse, thinking that if she led, Erin might follow.

Erin looked at Mac, shaking her head. "This is bananas," she said with a goofy laugh, getting out of the car.

Mac smiled. She was her mother's daughter after all.

Erin put money in the meter and they walked the few paces over to Urth. "Hey, Erin, one last thing," Mac said timidly, because she was already racking up major favor-debt. "Could you maybe ditch the earrings? Totally not Adrienne."

Erin touched the peacock feathers hanging off her face and slipped them off. "Done." She took the Princess Leia buns out of her hair as well, and Mac sighed gratefully.

Just as Mac was about to explain the nuances of the situation to Erin, she spotted Emily on the patio of Urth, waving to her. Mac took a deep breath and reminded herself that powerful agents don't get stressy. Or at least they don't let it show.

"Okay, Erin. That's my star. For the next fifteen minutes, you're Adrienne!"

Mac strolled confidently to the metal table where Emily was seated with a woman who had to be her mom and a random girl. They were drinking raspberry iced teas and sharing a grilled chicken sandwich cut into thirds.

"Hey Mac!" Emily said, flashing her lightbulb smile. "This is my mom, Lori, and this is my best friend, Paige." She pointed to a girl who was a chubby version of herself. Mac shook hands with Lori and surveyed Emily's bestie.

Emily and Paige were wearing the exact same outfit: homemade denim cutoffs with checkered fabric sewn to the bottom. They wore red tank tops with the same checkered fabric tied in a bow to one sleeve. They'd clearly sewn these monstrosities themselves. *Um, note to everyone*, Mac thought. *Unless you're Stella McCartney, don't make your own clothes.*

"You girls are like twins," Mac deadpanned.

"Yeah, but we're *so not!*" Paige laughed as though

it were funny. Her voice was a touch too loud, and she was one of those people who snorted when they giggled. Clearly *this* was the bad influence on Emily. Mac noticed that Paige was also wearing a Mandy Moore pin (a joke?), a blue-and-white polka-dot headband in her frizzy hair, and big oversize red beads à la *Sex and the City*.

"It makes us laugh to dress alike," Emily said softly.

Mac decided the topic of them dressing the same was making her nauseated and chose to move on. "I'd like to introduce you to Adrienne Little-Armstrong, the first female partner at Initiative Agency."

Emily shot Mac a confused glance, but Mac gave her a go-with-it look.

They sat down on the wrought-iron patio chairs across the table. Paige and Emily nodded in unison. Lori looked perplexed, keeping her eyes on Erin as they shook hands.

"I'm sorry, Adrienne," Lori said as she regained control of her hand. She reached for the ceramic salt-shaker. "It's just that you're not what I expected. You look so young."

"It's the salt!" Erin exclaimed. "Totally removed salt from my diet, took ten years off."

Lori put the saltshaker back in the middle of the wooden table.

"And a successful life in Bel-Air, that also keeps me young," she added, nodding enthusiastically.

Mac realized this was her window back into the conversation. "Yes. Speaking of Bel-Air . . . We feel that Emily has what it takes to succeed in this town," Mac said in her most professional voice, looking at Lori. "You've done a great job with her," she added, remembering that mothers love to hear great things about their children.

"Let's circle back on that one," Erin said, making an air circle with her index finger. "How would you like to go to the top?" Erin said, pointing upward with her pointer finger.

"Sounds good to me," Emily nodded. She looked at Mac again, who nodded back.

"'Cause that's where I take people. The *top*." Erin pointed at the sky again and whispered *top* like it was a secret hideout.

A waitress came to their table and Erin ordered a soy latte. Mac asked for a water with lemon, hoping to keep the meeting short. She needed to get Lori sold on the idea before Erin said anything else insane.

"We actually already have a part in mind." Mac turned to Lori, who put down her third of the chicken sandwich. "It's the role of a lifetime, oppo-site Davey Woodward. It's in Emily's wheelhouse," Mac said, channeling her inner Adrienne. She leaned into the table, the wood brushing her bare forearms. "We'd like to represent her," Mac lied, substituting the *we* for *I* in her head.

"I have a few questions," Paige said, popping annoyingly back into the conversation like a call-waiting beep. "Will you be charging Emily for head-shots? Or for representation?" Her chubby hands were clasped and propping up her chin.

Someone's been reading the *I Know Nothing About L.A. Handbook*, Mac thought. But she had to be polite. "Anyone who tries to take money from a client is a scam artist. We only *take* money when you *make* money."

Paige nodded triumphantly, as though she'd just done her friend a great service. The waitress reappeared with Erin's latte and Mac's water. Erin eagerly took a sip.

Lori Mungler cleared her throat. "What kind of a role is this?"

Just then Mac's phone rang. Coco's face popped up on her iPhone screen, and she immediately hit ignore. "Excuse me, that's a client," she said impor-tantly.

"It's the role of a *lifetime*," Erin said, putting her latte down and using her secret-hideout-voice again. "Think of No Doubt without Gwen Stefani. Up to now your life has been No Doubt and you're about to be No Doubt with Gwen Stefani. And then in a few years you can go solo, marry that hottie, have a kid, and name him Kingston."

"What Adrienne means"—Mac wished she could make Erin stop talking—"is that this is a star-making role." Mac's phone buzzed again. This time Coco was texting her. BIG NEWS! it read. WHERE R U? Mac glanced down at her phone but quickly returned her focus to the table.

"I only work with stars," Erin said. "I don't bust my buns to get people one-liners on bad shows. If you want that, go to the Valley and stand in line for some B level agent."

Mac cleared her throat and drew her chair closer to the table. "It's a great script. A girl pretends to be a boy in order to get into a great boarding school. Classic with an edge. All we need from Emily is one week."

"Do you have a contract?" Paige inserted herself again.

It was actually a good point, Mac thought, annoyed. But of course she didn't have one, so she took another tack. "Actually, Paige, contracts are for when Emily gets the role."

Paige nodded smugly, adjusting her polka-dot headband. The pattern clashed with the checkered bow on her shoulder.

Mac's phone lit up uh-gain with Coco's face. Three communication attempts in five minutes meant breaking news. "Excuse me, I *have* to take this." Mac brought her phone to her ear. "Talk to me," she answered.

"O-M-G, you are never going to believe what is happening to me *this week!*" Coco screamed. "I have an audition with Brigham Powell! *Brigham Powell!*"

This call could not have come at a better time. "That's right, you've got an audition with Brigham Powell," Mac replied evenly, as though she'd arranged it herself.

"Hellooooo? Could you be a little more excited for me?" Coco said. Mac made a mental note to readdress this topic with ten times more enthusiasm the next time she saw Coco. But for now, she had to sound like an agent in front of Team Emily.

"Brigham Powell?" Erin said excitedly. "He's launched every major pop star in the past ten years," she told Lori. Her enthusiasm was genuine. "Coco has a meeting with him?"

"I'm in a meeting," Mac said into the phone. Their waitress hovered within earshot, clearly hoping for some Hollywood gossip. "We'll discuss this later?"

"But there's more—" Coco began.

"Talk soon." *Click.* Mac reminded herself that it was for the greater good. She powered down her phone and returned her attention to the table. She looked directly at Lori. "So what do you say?"

"I'm not sure," Lori said slowly. All eyes on the table zoomed in on her. Even their waitress and a couple in matching aviators and James Perse T-shirts seemed to be waiting for an answer. "They always say whatever you think about most will come to you, but this is all very new to me—"

"Oh my gosh, how much do you looooove *The Secret?*" Erin exclaimed, forgetting her Adrienne persona and leaning forward eagerly.

"You've read it?" Lori asked, her face softening.

"Read it? I give it to all my friends. It changed my life. And yes, you absolutely did put this into the universe. It's the law of attraction." For the first time that lunch, Lori looked relaxed.

"Okay, one week it is." Lori smiled.

"Thank you, thank you, thank you, thank you!" Emily jumped up to hug Lori. Paige smiled like a third-grader.

Erin brought her hands up to make a camera and faked snapping a picture. "Kodak moment!" she exclaimed.

"Now we get you camera-ready," Mac said to Emily. "We'll have her back by eight." Mac stood up to shake Lori's hand.

Erin took one last sip of her soy latte. "Oh. And I know this is so like two hours ago, but another thing is dairy. When you cut out dairy, it's like saying hello to a new life."

Mac didn't interrupt Erin's dairy rant—her plan was working. She could read her future like an *Us Weekly* horoscope: Emily would get the role, Mac would get social chair, and they'd both be famous and live happily ever after.

Life was easy when you knew how to make it happen. Or, as Erin would say, when you knew what you wanted and put it into the universe.

CHAPTER FourTeen

Emily's L.A. Itinerary

Wednesday, September 2

3 PM   Meet talent agent (eek!)

4 PM   Rest of the day/the future—???

8 PM   Back to Econo Lodge

Emily sat in the backseat of Mac's pretend-mom's Prius, sweating like she was in a spinning class, even under her knees.

"So . . ." Emily leaned between the driver's and passenger's seats. She expected Mac to explain what had just happened, but Mac just fluffed her long hair and inspected her makeup in the mirror. "What's going on?" Emily demanded, eyeing Erin.

Mac reached into her canvas Marc tote and pulled out a Red Bull. "Okay, here's the dealio. My mom's booked until this weekend and this role is gonna be gone by then. You remember Erin, my mother's personal assistant. She knows everything about her, so it's like having my mom around anyway."

"I'm totally Adrienne," Erin said. "But I'm Erin!" She winked at Emily in the rearview mirror.

Emily sat back and looked out the window. The streets were lined with palm trees. "Ohhh-kay."

"We're going to the Grove, in case you're wondering," Mac said, turning around to face the back. "It's a *mall*," she added, as though a mall were the most disgusting thing in the world. Emily knew better than to argue, but she also knew that to call the Grove a *mall* was like calling a Manolo a shoe. It was where Leonardo DiCaprio went to see movies and Jessica Biel went for Coffee Bean.

Mac shoved a giant Fred Segal shopping bag into the backseat. "You need to wear these clothes," she said. Emily's heart raced at the thought of what fabulous outfit might be in the bag. Did agents always bring clothes for new clients?

She tore the bag open eagerly only to have her heart sink at the contents: Abercrombie & Fitch jeans, Stanford baseball cap, and a Diesel button-down shirt. *Boys'* clothes.

"Is this a joke?" Emily asked.

"If you're going to play a boy"—Mac looked at Emily very seriously "you have to be so good at being a boy that the world can't catch you acting."

Emily stared at the pile of dirty clothes. The jeans

were wrinkled and looked like they'd been recently worn.

"And there's no better way to do it than in my brother's smelly clothes. It's a good thing he left these in the trunk earlier when he went surfing."

Emily gaped at the dirty boy-clothes and Mac rolled her eyes. "Listen, we're lucky they're even still auditioning for this part. We have to act fast. If anyone asks, you're my cousin Jeff. If they buy it, you're one step closer to nailing that audition. If not, we need to strategize. *Capisce?*"

"I guess so," Emily said, eyeing the outfit as if it were alive and going to eat her.

"That's why it's called 'acting,' not 'dressing pretty all the time,'" Mac sighed.

Easy for Mac to say. She was dressed in a fitted Lisa Kline skirt from this month's *Lucky*.

Erin dropped them off in the parking lot and they made their way into the Grove's enormous outdoor shopping area. Emily tried not to be distracted by the designer storefronts or the gushing turrets of the fountain. A cheerful green trolley glided past them on its tracks, and Emily fought the urge to ask Mac if they could go for a ride.

"Go change," Mac said as they rounded the corner and stood in front of a Coffee Bean & Tea Leaf.

"It's like Starbucks, but one step up. Nobody goes to Starbucks here," Mac gestured at the coffee shop as if it needed an introduction.

Emily opened her mouth to tell Mac she knew all about the L.A. coffee shop hierarchy, but instead she went wordlessly into the bathroom to change. She emerged five minutes later, feeling silly as she passed the same people who'd seen her enter in her normal-fitting cutoffs and red tank top. No one seemed to notice though—they were all typing at screenplays on their laptops.

Mac made a beeline for Abercrombie, but Emily didn't follow. Not yet. She quickly ran a mental scan of the guys at the Grove. There was one, carrying his girlfriend's Barneys bags, dragging his Nikes like a toddler who wasn't allowed to go to the park. There was another dude, kicking his foot listlessly against the stone edge of the fountain as he talked on his cell phone. Emily shuffled her feet with an unfamiliar laziness to her step.

"What are you doing?" Mac said, turning around. She was already several steps ahead of Emily.

Emily ignored her and made a couple more adjustments. She shook her shoulders loosely, finding different angles for slouching until something clicked between her body and her brain and she knew she'd found the way "Jeff" would walk. She hung her head back, her chin jutting out from beneath her baseball cap, and let her hipbones guide her.

"Got it," Emily said, and clapped her hands together once. That was what her best guy friend, Sean Shea, did whenever he'd made a decision, like ordering double onion pizza or buying the Tony Hawk video game.

"O-M-G! Is this how you work? I heart it so much," Mac squealed. "You're totally method acting!"

Emily nodded once with her chin, just like Sean. Enough of this girly chitchat. It was fun to think she could just ignore people if she wanted to, like guys from Iowa who thought they were cool.

As Emily stepped into the over-air-conditioned store, she realized this felt just like last night, when she sneaked into Davey Woodward's party. She puffed out her chest, hung her head low, and instantly felt like she was seeing through Jeff's eyes.

She'd left Emily waiting at the fountain outside the store.

Normally she'd have headed straight for the sundresses, but today she shuffled toward the boys' jeans. She told herself that she had to get a new pair since she'd ripped her other ones skateboarding. Emily was browsing the different washes when a pretty salesgirl with a fake-'n'-bake tan came up to her and said sweetly, "Let me know if you need these in another size."

Emily nodded but said nothing, and the girl went back to folding polos. She didn't seem weirded out. In fact, she didn't seem to notice anything. Could it actually be *working*?

There was only one way to find out.

Emily walked up confidently to the men's changing rooms.

"Yo, can I try these on?" Emily asked in a low, scratchy voice, hoisting the jeans at the girl. She didn't make direct eye contact—Jeff wouldn't do that.

"Sure," the girl said finally, and went to unlock a cabin. "My name's Angie."

"Cool," Emily said, in a guttural, no-emotion voice. She stepped into the changing room and the salesgirl closed the door behind her. Emily's heart was beating with nervous excitement. It was really working! Plus, she'd never been in a guys' changing room before.

Just then, the salesgirl tapped at the door. "Oh, one more thing—"

Emily's heart beat faster. Had her hips given her away? Had she spoken too much like a girl? Was she going to get thrown out of Abercrombie?

"We also have them in a darker rinse. Just lemme me know if you need anything."

"Uh, thanks," Emily called over the top of the stall door, doing her absolute best to hide the girly enthusiasm that was filling her whole body. She leaned her forehead against the cool wooden slats of the changing-room door and stayed there for at least fifty seconds, long enough to try on a pair of pants.

When she emerged, just to prove to herself and Mac that it hadn't been a fluke, she handed the jeans back to Angie. "Nah, but thanks," she said.

Angie took the pants, her head tilted to the side. "Bye-eeeeee," she said in a high, flirty voice.

Mac grabbed Emily's forearm possessively and dragged her toward a stack of green and brown cashmere sweaters. "Nice work." She grinned, dropping Emily's arm. "Task one is complete!"

Emily wanted to jump up and down and hug Mac, but she was:

1.   Afraid to wrinkle her. And . . .
2.   Afraid of blowing her cover.

She settled for a Jeff-worthy head nod.

"Let's get out of here. I need to get you home." Mac gestured toward the front of the store. The sun was setting behind the half-naked mannequins in the window.

"Mac!"

They spun around to face a girl in a pink tennis skirt with brown hair pulled into low pigtails with pink ribbons. The ensemble was a slow death by pink.

"Mac!" the girl squealed again, trotting over for an air kiss.

"Hi, Kimmie," Mac said evenly.

"So are you totally psyched for my b-day par-tay?" Kimmie asked, not waiting for an answer. "DJ AM called to confirm today." She spotted a pink cardigan on a white shelf next to them and tossed it over her arm without looking at the cut or size.

"Great, great." Mac nodded noncommittally.

Emily decided to stay quiet in case Mac wanted to keep their little project under wraps. There was awkward silence while Kimmie scanned "Jeff" like a bar code.

Gulp.

"We're just shopping." Mac took a step in front of Emily as though trying to block her from Kimmie's view. Emily imagined Kimmie telling everyone at Mac's school that she was friends with a cross-dresser. "'Cause that's what people do, just shop, you know." She shrugged and pushed her wooden bangles down to her wrist.

Kimmie peered curiously around Mac to get another glimpse of Emily. She crinkled her nose. Emily ignored her and pretended to be supremely interested in a pair of flared trouser jeans on the display next to them. Mac took a deep breath, clearly waiting for Kimmie to go.

"He's cute," Kimmie stage-whispered, flashing her eyes in Emily's direction.

Mac blinked twice, suddenly realizing the "him" was Emily. "Oh, sorry, that's just Jeff." She waved dismissively. "He's my—"

"You go, girl." Kimmie cheerfully interrupted. "If you want to bring him to my party Friday, that's cool. 'Cause my Aunt Barbara called and she broke her hip, so she can't come." She shrugged her pink-clad shoulders.

"Yeah, sure," Mac said without missing a beat.

"Great. See you then. Both of you!" Kimmie gave Jeff a wink.

Emily and Mac watched as Kimmie walked away, her pigtails bobbing. When Kimmie's pink tennis skirt had vanished from view, Mac turned to Emily, her hands on the hips of her Lisa Kline skirt.

"Brah-vo. You just fooled the Tawker, the biggest gossip in school. She's an extremely important person to know. Her dad, like, owns this town."

Emily gave Mac another casual Jeff nod. But inside she was bursting with the feeling of good things to come.

She was ready.

Look out Hollywood, here I come!

FIFTEEN

becks

◀ Thursday   September 3 ▶

7 AM Rise and shine

11 AM Hang w/ Dad

2 PM Makeover/Shop/Whatever Mac has me
booked for

3 PM Mac's photo-op

Becks and her dad, Clutch, were tossing around a football on the beach. It was noon on a gorgeous late-summer day, and the Malibu shore was crowded with colorful umbrellas and blankets filled with Los Angelenos soaking up the sun. Her dad spiraled the brown ball through the air. Becks chased after it mindlessly. She was there but she wasn't *there* there. As she caught the football and brought it into her Roxy bikini–clad body, she was thinking of Austin.

She was in the Goal Zone, when she couldn't stop herself from obsessing about her goals. She often got that way before a major surfing competition, spending hours visualizing herself riding the waves. It worked in surfing. Hopefully it would work on Austin.

Then Mac's voice pierced through the zone. *Ruf-Ruf!*

"Um, Dad, can I ask you a question?" Becks sighed, turning the ball in circles between her fingertips. She moved toward him across the sand. "It's about boys."

"Boys?" Clutch looked at Becks as if she'd made up the word. He scratched his head and twirled a finger through his gray-flecked brown hair. At thirty-nine, Clutch Becks still had the same rugged good looks that had attracted a female audience to his boy-centric prank show. He was tall and rangy and liked to complain about how old he was getting, even though he still looked and acted like a teenager. His favorite expression was "Oh, my aching bones," which he'd cry in a creaky old-lady voice as he surfed a wave or dove for a football or did other things that suggested his bones were not aching in the least.

"What do you need boys for? Boys ruin everything," he said definitively, leaning over, panting. He rested his hands on his red-and-white floral-print Quiksilver board shorts.

"Well, really it's just one boy." Becks dragged a toe through the sand.

"That's even worse," Clutch said, straightening up and shaking some sand out of his green Crocs. "Stick to your girlfriends," he finished.

Becks stared at the sand. This conversation was heading down the highway to Awkwardville. She jogged backward, throwing her dad a perfect pass. They tossed the football back and forth a few more times, and then a dog leaped up and grabbed the ball from the air.

Ruf-ruf!

Boone barked again, and Becks looked up to see Austin wearing a new Rusty T-shirt that matched his blue-gray eyes. He grabbed the ball from Boone's mouth and threw it back. The heavy football spiraled through the air.

And then it slammed into her face.

Becks fell onto the sand, not sure which hurt more: the pain in her face or the embarrassment of looking like a total tool in front of her crush.

"Dude, you all right?" Austin's head appeared above her, blocking out the sun. His shaggy hair hung down, framing his tanned face. "You look like you might hurl."

"Evie!" Clutch appeared on her other side, calling Becks by the girly nickname he only used on special occasions. "You okay?"

Becks nodded. Her head was spinning. Her lip was throbbing. Boone licked her ear.

Clutch smiled once he saw she was going to

be all right. "You really flew a few feet back there! Would've made the gag reel on *That Was Clutch*, at the very least." He nodded approvingly.

"Hey, we should get some ice on that," Austin said, nodding at her quickly swelling lip. He helped her up with a strong hand. As she stood upright, Becks felt dizzy, like she really *might* hurl. "I've got some ice in my cooler, I'll go grab some," he offered.

But Becks was already running into the house and away from Austin. "I'm okay," she screamed without looking back. "No worries!" Her lip was already so swollen that it came out *No worrith*.

She tramped up the wooden steps to the deck and grabbed the steel handle of the sliding glass door. Before she could even get the door open, she caught sight of her massively swollen lip in its shiny reflection. There was no makeup that could cover that up. Mac was going to murder her, starting with her puffy mouth.

Her dad was right about one thing: Boys really did ruin everything.

CHAPTER
SIXTEEN

Emily's L.A. Itinerary

Thursday, September 3

2 PM   Makeover!

4 PM   Rest of the day???

E mily sat in the backseat of the Prius as Erin steered the girls down La Cienega Boulevard. Mac slipped a giant pair of Gucci aviators over her face, her blond mane spilling over the headrest. Emily was too confused to relax. Again and again she came back to the question, *Why me?*

"You okay back there?" Mac asked without turning around or opening her eyes. Her aviators hid everything.

"I guess I just don't understand *why* you're doing this," Emily said, staring at the back of Mac's head. After channeling "Jeff" at the Grove yesterday, Emily had been wondering what was in it for Mac, anyway?

"Think of me as your fairy godmother. I give you a career and then I take 10 percent." Finally, she turned to face Emily and pulled her sunglasses down her ski-jump nose, giving a cute wink. She slipped the aviators back on and turned to face the front again. "Welcome to Rodeo Drive, Emily," Mac said proudly, as though she owned it.

Emily glanced down Via Rodeo, which was open only to foot traffic. The street was paved in small black bricks that fanned out in a beautiful pattern. Potted plants rested in the middle of the blocked-off street, and the occasional palm tree sprouted from the sidewalk. A stately gray marble entryway read TIFFANY & CO. The La Perla sign was a gold plaque.

Erin stopped the car in front of a small boutique with yellow awnings. "Follow me," Mac said to Emily as she hopped out of the silver car. "Erin, can you be back here in about two hours?"

"Right-o." Erin saluted the girls.

The yellow awning read, FRÉDÉRIC FEKKAI, and Emily's breath caught in her throat. This was the hair salon where Mischa Barton and Sienna Miller went.

"Mac . . ." She lowered her voice. "I can't pay for this."

Mac smiled an almost-evil grin and slowly reached into her canvas Marc tote, pulling out an American Express card. "That's what this is for."

When they got out of the elevator, Mac breezed past two girls at the counter and sashayed to the

Spanish-style outdoor veranda that overlooked Beverly Hills. Becks and Coco were already lounging on forest-green pillows and drinking Pellegrinos with lime. Becks was wearing board shorts and flip-flops, and Coco had on a fluttery white wrap dress.

"Whatup, ladies?" Becks said, lifting up her Ray-Bans and putting down her copy of *Cosmopolitan*. She had a stack of women's magazines on her lap, which she appeared to be dog-earing and highlighting. Her lip was swollen like she'd been stung by a bee. Make that several bees. She'd slathered gloss all over her lip, seemingly to detract attention from the swelling, but the sunshine reflected off her mouth like moonlight on the ocean.

Mac froze and Emily almost knocked into her. "Becks. What. The. Heck. Happened?"

"Missed a football." Becks shrugged.

"You're the most coordinated person I know," Mac said, stunned. "You don't miss."

Becks stared at the patio floor but said nothing.

The silence was broken as a man with a dyed-black bowl haircut walked over and stood in front of Mac. "Gianni!" she cried excitedly, wrapping him in a hug. He looked like Wilma from *Scooby-Doo*, except he was wearing a black satin corset.

"Is-ah-thees our star?" he asked, pulling away and rubbing Emily's cheeks.

"She *will be* our star once you're through with her," Mac said proudly. "Emily, this is Gianni. He's from Milan."

Gianni curtsied and pulled Emily back inside the cavernous salon. The room was lined with oversize mirrors and green leather salon chairs. He seated her next to a circular window and whisked a comb from the back pocket of his skinny white jeans. "I'm ah-going to make you *eeeen-credible*," he whispered, as though it were a threat. Then he turned to his timid assistant. "Vash 'er and bring 'er back to me!"

An hour later, Gianni was folding aluminum foil into Emily's hair for lowlights. She'd never been so pampered. The longest haircut she'd ever had before had been at Kut N' Kurl, and that had taken twenty-five minutes.

Emily was studying herself in the gold-framed mirror, wondering what she would look like when the foil came off, when a very skinny woman with Jolly Rancher–red hair appeared in the mirror.

"I'm your makeup artist," the woman said in a gruff voice. "Salome."

Salome had very pale skin, a very high ponytail, and very purple eyeliner. She looked like a Picasso from his Cubist years. Without warning, Salome pulled out a can of Evian water and began spritzing Emily's face. She blinked.

"You have gor-geous skin," Salome said, over-*enun*-ciating every word, the way people do when they are angry and trying to stay calm. "I'm going to apply some Chanel base to even out your skin," she said.

Technically, Emily wasn't supposed to wear makeup, though she planned to re-negotiate this rule anyway. What was eighth grade for if you couldn't wear mascara?

Just then Becks barged over. "Are you guys doing makeup?" she asked, a silly question, since Salome was obviously brushing Emily's eyelids with something. "I'm gonna watch," Becks said, hovering next to Mac.

Salome took one look at Becks and honed in on her puffy lip. "You look like Angelina Jolie," she purred.

Mac regarded her friend again, one hand on her wide-leg-jeaned hip. "Okay, I guess it's not *so* bad."

Becks's face flushed. She touched her lip and smiled gratefully at Salome.

"I *liiiike*," Salome said, reaching over a table with hundreds of iridescent powders and glistening glosses. "I'm brushing a pale white eyeshadow over your eyes," Salome went on. Emily closed her eyes and felt the feathery brush tickle her face. "Like headlights to your face."

Salome and Gianni pushed, pulled, combed, and brushed her for another hour. Emily summoned all her willpower to not peek at herself in the mirror. Finally, once Salome had dabbed the second coat of coral lip gloss on Emily's lips, and Gianni had sprayed Frédéric Fekkai protective sealant on her hair, Mac took her hand.

"Emily," Mac said, sounding like she was about to cry, "you came into this salon Ashlee Simpson circa 2004, and you are about to leave looking like Rachel Bilson post-*O.C.*" Mac spun Emily's chair around so that she faced the mirror. "Open your eyes," Mac commanded.

Emily had to blink several times to convince herself that the girl she saw in the mirror was really her. It *was* amazing. Her hair was back to its natural cinnamon color. Loose, sideswept bangs framed her brown eyes. Her dark eyelashes were long and dewy, her cheeks were rosy, her lips were plump and shiny. She *glowed*. And yet . . . she looked like herself. The best version of herself that had ever existed.

"Ta-da!" Mac turned to Emily an hour later. They were standing with Becks and Coco in front of a white, ivy-covered hacienda. "Welcome to the only place you'll ever need to shop again. It's called Fred Segal, and it's where everyone who's anyone shops."

Of course Emily knew Fred Segal. It was the reason she and Paige had saved their babysitting allowance. All around them were the designer names Emily and Paige quizzed each other on from *Lucky* and *InStyle*. Chip & Pepper. Yaya. Ron Herman. Free People. She wanted to spend hours trying on those clothes, just seeing what she would look like in the same brands that the stars wore.

A young brunette was heading into the baby-clothes section. "That looks like Maggie Gyllenhaal," Emily whispered to Coco.

"That *is* Maggie Gyllenhaal," Coco said, laughing.

Emily picked up a plain cotton henley with pink stitching. $138.

Mac grabbed her elbow and led her to a staircase. "Rack shopping is for amateurs. Let's go."

At the top of the stairs, a woman with a blond Afro wearing a Diane von Furstenberg wrap dress greeted Mac with a hug and ushered the girls into a private suite. The dressing room was wallpapered with ivory-and-gold damask wallpaper. Gold-tasseled curtains divided up changing sections, and the floor was covered with dozens of overlapping Persian carpets.

"Marianne, we have a party tomorrow night that will determine our Q rating," Mac said, stepping into the center of the room. "Kimmie Tachman is having her Sweet Thirteen."

"Only three birthdays away from her nose job," Marianne singsonged, and winked at the girls.

Mac turned to Emily. "Kimmie's the one who thinks you're a guy," she explained, as though Emily would have forgotten meeting Elliot Tachman's daughter.

Marianne motioned to the oversize gold chaise. The four girls sat.

"Just you?" Marianne asked Mac.

"All of us," Mac replied.

"Absolutely." Marianne nodded. She stood in front of Emily, taking her in critically, like an art student attempting to understand a Jackson Pollock painting. Finally she spoke. "You're one of those girls who can wear every color but khaki. I'm jealous."

"Color envy," Coco agreed solemnly. "I can't wear green."

Emily nodded, not sure whether she was supposed to say thank you. Marianne mumbled a few words into an intercom on the wall. Seconds later, several model-looking women waltzed toward the girls with four racks of pretty clothes, one rack per girl, and several stacks of shoeboxes.

Emily's rack was stacked with brands like Marc Jacobs, K2, Chloé, and Yellowfield 8. They were all just the right fit for her tiny size-two frame. Becks's and Coco's racks were lined with Philosophy and Robert Rodriguez dresses. Mac reviewed her picks: Tracy Reese. Karta. Just Cavalli. Even though Emily had never actually *touched* a Marni dress, *Vogue* had taught her well.

"Let's get to work!" Mac clapped her hands. Marianne hit a button on a remote control, and Justin Timberlake's "SexyBack" blared in the room while the girls began trying on their endless array of very expensive, very snug, very beautiful dresses.

Mac squeezed into a one-shoulder D&G silk dress. She turned to the left and then to the right and then she gave the dress back to the salesgirl.

Coco stepped in front of the three-way mirror, examining herself in a black sequined Tracey Reese trapeze dress.

"Thanks for showing us what happens when sequins attack." Mac giggled.

"I like this," Coco said defensively, swirling around to check out her rear view.

"O-M-G!" Mac said, hitting herself lightly on the head. "We totally need to discuss your dance partner. Didn't you find out who she is yesterday?"

Coco paused and bit her super-shined lip. "Actually . . ." she began, shaking out her long, chocolate-colored hair. "Actually, it was no one famous. Just a nobody."

"Cardammon didn't get you Tisdale?" Mac asked as she shimmied into a leaf-green YSL cocktail dress.

"Nah, just some random." Coco ran her hands along the sequins on the hem of the dress. She seemed nervous.

"Peeps, what do we think of this?" Becks interjected, waving her arms look-at-me style. She had on a strapless pink zebra-print dress that stopped mid-thigh.

"Um, Becks, it's a *birthday* party, not a bachelor party. Lift your arms," Mac instructed.

Becks did, and the dress rose just enough to reveal her pale blue American Apparel boy briefs.

"I rest my case." Mac nodded smugly. She turned to put the green YSL dress back on the rack, spotted Emily, and gasped. Her hands flew to her chest.

Emily mentally braced herself for whatever insult was about to knock her down.

"I love it," Mac said, in that teary voice that

actresses use in thank-you speeches at the Academy Awards.

"T.C.," Coco agreed. "Too cute! There should be a word for 'so cute it hurts,' because you are so cute it hurts!"

Emily looked in the mirror. She was wearing a gold-and-silver Cavalli disco dress that made her A-cups look like B's and her legs look supermodel-long. She smiled.

"Normally I'd say you don't marry the first dress that fits, but sometimes you get lucky. *That* is a keeper." Mac nodded, pointing up and down at Emily's lean frame.

"Totes," Becks said matter-of-factly. She'd given up and tucked the pink dress into her boy shorts.

"One more thing," Mac said, reaching over to Emily. "I only do this because I care." In one quick movement, she yanked off Emily's BFF bracelet.

"But—" Emily began.

"Emily, friends don't let friends wear outfit-wrecking accessories," Mac said, reaching for an aquamarine Tracy Reese. Then she smiled like a proud mom. "Now, look at yourself, you're good to go. Welcome to Hollywood, Emily Mungler!"

"Your last name is *Mungler*?" Becks asked. She

said *Mungler* like she was reading *bratwurst* on a menu. She took a seat on the chaise.

"Becks is right," Mac said sternly. She looked Emily's reflection square in the face. "It has to go."

"*What*?" Emily cried, suddenly protective over something she'd never given that much thought to.

"Think about it. Your fame-name will be E-Mu. More like Ew. Big Ew," Mac pointed out.

"Mungler the Bungler," Coco said.

"MuMu," Becks added.

Emily looked at Mac, her jaw forming a hard line. Sure, *Mungler* wasn't the most beautiful name, but it was hers. "No one judges you by your name," Emily said defensively, resting her hands on her hips.

"Sure," Mac agreed easily, pulling the bodice of the blue dress over her chest. "I'm sure Diane Belmont, Tara Patrick, Demetria Guynes, and Eilleen Edwards would agree."

"*Who*?" Emily faltered.

"You know them as Lucille Ball, Carmen Electra, Demi Moore, and Shania Twain." Mac coolly smoothed the micropleats of her Tracy Reese. "*They* obviously thought names were important."

Emily looked at her reflection in the three-way

mirror. The sparkles of the disco dress cast a golden glow over her features.

"Okay, so let's figure this out," Mac said, as though Emily had agreed. She rubbed her temples and began uttering sounds under her breath, like she was casting a spell. "Actually, what's your middle name?"

"Skyler," Emily said. "I know it's sort of cheesy together, Emily Skyler Mungler, but my mom really—"

"Done," Mac said triumphantly, cutting her off. "I revise my last statement. Welcome to Hollywood, Emily *Skyler*!"

"Oooooh, nice!" Coco nodded.

"Sweet," Becks agreed.

"You're really serious about this?" Emily asked in disbelief.

The four girls stood in a row in front of the wall-to-wall, floor-to-ceiling mirror. Their cocktail dresses glittered and shimmered and probably cost more than Emily's entire ten-day trip to Los Angeles.

Mac took another glance at Emily's reflection. "*Now* you are ready for your close-up! Remember, one foot in front, hips to the side," Mac instructed through a stewardess smile, assuming the position.

"Wait, what are you—" Emily started to say.

But before she could finish, Mac marched out of

the dressing room, down the stairs, and toward the front door, and the other girls followed. Mac handed her AmEx to Marianne in one fluid motion. As soon as they emerged from Fred Segal's ivy-covered façade, a man all dressed in black popped up from behind a black Mercedes.

Instead of running away, Mac arched her back, pointed one foot in front of the other, and pivoted her hips. Without a second's delay, the other girls assumed the same position, wordlessly arranging themselves so no one blocked anyone else. Emily followed their cue while the man walked around them, snapping pictures.

"Her name is Emily Skyler," Mac told the paparazzo. "She's going to be the next big thing."

"Thanks, ladies," he said, after snapping several more photos.

Mac brushed her hands together as though she'd just finished a laborious task. Then she surveyed her friends. "It's nice to be noticed when we look our best," she noted, fluffing her hair for extra oomph. "Now, back inside. We've got to get you some L.A. basics, Emily Skyler."

Emily Skyler. It was sort of pretty, actually. It *did* sound like a star's name. Emily was starting to believe that she really could be one, too.

CHAPTER
seventeen

mac

◀ Thursday   September 3 ▶

2 PM   Makeover

5 PM   Social chair strategy session

11 PM Beauty sleep (must look good for
       Kimmie's)

As Mac slouched into her clear green Pinkberry chair, she felt a tiny surge of relief that Emily was gone, deposited back at her hotel. Mac imagined it was how girls who had to get babysitting jobs felt when they were done with a shift: a tiny bit freer.

She and the girls were stopping at Pinkberry for fro-yo (obvi), but more importantly to discuss social chair strategy. It was necessary and crucial to establish a plan ASAP.

"So, girls," Mac began, spooning the mango topping out of her plain yogurt. "What did we think of our star?"

Becks shrugged. It took a lot for Becks to say anything very good or very bad about anyone. She just didn't have the gene that made you like gossip.

"I like her," Coco said. "She has that *je ne sais*

quoi." Coco waved her green-tea-fro-yo-coated spoon in the air.

Mac couldn't have said it better herself.

"*Très bien*," Mac agreed. She reached into her Marc Jacobs tote for her iBook. "I prepared a slide show of winning social chair campaigns of the past decade." She opened her white laptop so it faced her two best friends. Mac had pulled together this presentation the night she returned from New Adventures. She'd even set it to one of her favorite songs, "Oooh La La."

Mac booted up the slide show, and Becks and Coco leaned forward eagerly to look.

Across the laptop screen, the words BEL-AIR MIDDLE SCHOOL SOCIAL CHAIR: A HISTORICAL AND STATISTICAL ANALYSIS dissolved into a still shot of the school. It was an enormous, Spanish-style mansion with a terra-cotta-tiled roof, and bougain-villeas growing from the classroom's window boxes. The camera zoomed in on three girls seated on the school's blue-tiled front steps: 2004 SC winner Hay-lee Parda sat with her two BFFs, her first platinum album in her lap. It was enough to excuse their scarily outdated hip-slung belts.

"I forgot Haylee Parda got elected the day her record deal was announced," Coco said. "I thought she was *sooo* cool."

Haylee's glowing face pixilated and dissolved, and suddenly the frame was filled with a new image: Kira Simpson. She was hanging out of the passenger seat of her mom's silver convertible CLK signing an autograph. She'd starred opposite Orlando Bloom in the adaptation of *A Tale of Two Cities* before graduating early from high school and going to Brown.

Next up was Emily Seierstad, grinning from the LCD screen with her over-bleached teeth. She'd written a thinly veiled roman à clef about being raised in Beverly Hills that had spent ten weeks on the *New York Times* best-sellers list.

Mac snapped her iBook closed. "As you can see, 100 percent of previously elected social chairs have succeeded beyond their school responsibilities. This is not just a popularity contest, although clearly that helps," she added. "So . . . I need to make sure everybody knows that I rock, starting with my campaign slogan. I'm looking for the cooler version of *I made Emily Skyler a star, and I'll make BAMS shine too.* Any ideas?"

Before Coco or Becks could even open their mouths to brainstorm, Mac felt two freakishly cold hands on her shoulders. She jerked back in surprise.

"Hey, girls," said an all-too familiar baby voice.

Mac's jaw stiffened. She swiveled in the green plastic chair to face her nemesis. Ruby wore tight Rock & Republic jeans with a white cropped James Perse tee. Kimmie Tachman stood protectively to Ruby's side in a pink Betsey Johnson taffeta dress, holding both of their yogurts, assistant-style.

"I know you didn't ask for my advice," Ruby cooed in that baby voice. "But I couldn't help overhear you discussing your campaign strategy—you know, your little star?" She made air quotes around *star* with her death-hands. "I thought I should tell you that Anastasia Caufield is interested in *Deal with It* after all."

Mac shot Kimmie a look, cocking one eyebrow.

"Well, I don't know if I heard right, and who knows if that's true," Kimmie said, shifting her weight from one foot to the other. "But I'm pretty sure my dad mentioned that auditions were closed."

Kimmie was a lot of things, but she wasn't fact-retarded. To be BAMS' top gossip, you had to have a high rate of correct intel; otherwise you were just a non-connected nobody with a vivid imagination.

"It's interesting you say that," Mac said, licking her neon-pink spoon slowly. Then she shrugged, leaving them to wonder what she meant by that.

"You guys, I better go," Kimmie said, glancing at her red NV phone—they didn't sell it in pink. "Last-minute huddle with the caterer. I'll see you at my party. *Hakuna matata*." Kimmie awkwardly tried to hand one of the yogurts she was holding to Ruby, who waved it off.

Mac rolled her eyes that Kimmie had just quoted *Lion King* not-ironically in public. It was a testament to just how big a deal her dad was that anyone talked to her at all. Minus the Hollywood royalty status, Kimmie was just a musical theater nerd who abused the color pink.

Ruby smiled Mona Lisa–style at Mac. "Well, I guess I should get going too." She looked right at Coco. "See *you* later, babe."

Coco looked down at her green-tea frozen yogurt, which was now just a melting pea-colored liquid.

"Did you just call her *babe*?" Mac asked.

Ruby smirked. "Don't be jealous, *Macdaddy*. I guess I'll see all of you at Kimmie's party. Ciao for now."

Even the sight of Ruby's Rock & Republics making their way out of Pinkberry's sliding glass doors didn't make Mac feel better. There was something about Ruby that made her uneasy. It was genuine confidence, and Mac couldn't understand why Ruby had so much. What in the world did Ruby Goldman have up her cropped James Perse sleeve?

CHAPTER
EIGHTEEN

COCO

◄ Thursday   September 3 ►

2 PM   Makeover w/ I.C.; tell Mac big news?

5 PM   Pinkberry (if Mac hasn't killed me yet)

7 PM   Choose outfits for audition

Coco stood in front of a poster of a girl in a backless leotard and furry leg warmers at the American Apparel on Robertson Boulevard. She was there with Ruby and Cardammon with the goal of selecting their audition ensembles for Saturday. The plan was to choose basics, which Cardammon would accessorize with pieces from her H&M collection. "You need to look *cute*," Cardammon had explained. "But like you put *zero thought whatsoever* into looking cute, yeah?"

Cardammon also hoped that pictures of the girls might "accidentally" appear in tabloids that week so that Brigham would get the message these girls were already very interesting. Coco had wanted to tell Mac that she and her mom had the same idea with that Fred Segal photo-op, but then thought better of it. Coco had spent the entire Emily Mungler makeover session with sweaty palms and a nervous tickle in her throat. The thought of Mac finding out about her partnership with Ruby—let alone seeing it in a magazine—gave her the shivers.

As they browsed, photographers stood outside on the sidewalk in the growing darkness, pressing themselves firmly against the glass windows, snapping pictures of Cardammon. There were so many flashes that it seemed like the store had a strobe light. Coco tried to keep at least three feet between herself and Ruby as they whisked through the sleek white space, plucking items from the chrome racks of colorful clothing as they went. The other customers tried to look like they were shopping, but their sidelong gazes gave them away.

"Life in a fishbowl." Cardammon waved her ringed fingers at the horde of paparazzi outside the glass and sighed dramatically. "And remember this: If you don't give them what they want, they'll find the worst picture of you ever taken and use that instead. This way, everyone wins." She swiveled to face the photographers in her red-satin tube-top dress, offering them her best angle. Flashbulbs burst as a paparazzo took her picture. Then she turned back to Ruby and Cardammon as though it had never happened. "Well, my little stars, shall we?"

Coco sifted through a rack of leotards, barely making eye contact with Ruby.

"Girls, what do you think?" Cardammon held out a teal pencil micromini skirt and a neon yellow wifebeater. The skirt definitely wouldn't pass Mac's "raise your arms" test.

Neither Ruby nor Coco said anything.

"Got it." Cardammon nodded briskly, understanding the silence. "Too '80s. Let's try for something fresher." She went back to browsing the store, and Ruby and Coco followed behind.

"Ooooh, luvvies, what about *this*?" Cardammon held up blue cotton track shorts, the kind Coco wore under dresses. "You could wear them with thigh-high socks."

Ruby smiled. "Those ones with the blue stripes at the top!"

"Cheeky!" Cardammon clapped her hands.

Coco looked back and forth between her mother and Ruby in horror. These two really got each other. Coco knew that if she ever tried to explain to her mother why she didn't like Ruby, Cardammon would tell her that Jaqueline, her best friend, used to be her prime rival. Sometimes you hate someone because you actually *luv* them.

But that still didn't answer the Mac issue.

Coco was still trying to figure out how she could explain all this to Mac when a little girl came up to Cardammon. She wore Heidi-style braids and blue corduroy overalls and looked about seven years old.

"Would you please take a picture with me?" the girl whispered, trembling. Her face was bright red, and she had clearly summoned all her courage for this approach. Across the store, a father in an electric green American Apparel hoodie held up his iPhone.

Cardammon pretended to have a think. She put her hands on her hips and glanced coquettishly to the side before she smiled. "I will take *two* pictures with you." Although she never said yes to adults, she never said no to children.

Ruby and Coco stood beside a rack of stretchy terry-cloth dresses and watched while Cardammon sashayed over to the little girl's dad. Then, as though performing a perfectly choreographed dance move, the new duo turned and faced each other, arms crossed.

Ruby leaned in toward Coco. "So, *that* was interesting at Pinkberry. Let me guess: You didn't tell your BFF we're working together?"

"I didn't exactly have a lot of time to tell her," Coco hissed back.

Ruby smiled complacently. "Here's the thing,"

she said, pulling her hair into a low side pony and looking very much like an American Apparel model herself. "*Kimmie* knows about us."

Coco's heart sank. Telling Kimmie was like sending out a school-wide e-mail.

"Just giving you the heads-up," Ruby said, as if she were being truly helpful. And then, as if remembering to use her baby voice, she added, "'Cause who *knows* what'll come up at Kimmie's party."

Coco slowly set down the black tube dress she was holding, her hands shaking. The last thing she wanted was for Mac to hear she was working with Ruby from someone else, in an oh-so-public place. Noticing the flickering flashes of the paparazzi, she stepped away from Ruby.

"Oooh, I think they got some good shots of us." Ruby flashed Coco a fake smile as she stepped over to a display of pink and yellow cotton tees.

Before Coco could say anything, Cardammon returned holding an American Apparel shopping bag. "Luvvies, I made an executive decision," she said, pulling out silver lamé workout shorts, a striped jersey razor-backed tee, and opaque over-the-knee stockings.

Coco gaped.

Ruby squealed joyfully and clapped her hands.

Coco wasn't sure what was worse: the outfit or Ruby's reaction to it. The ensemble was a scary, too-revealing tribute to the '80s.

"Of course, we'll bedazzle it," Cardammon said matter-of-factly, surveying her purchases proudly.

"Of course," Ruby agreed, sounding like the sweetest girl in Los Angeles. She moved toward Cardammon and ran her fingers over the silver lamé.

Coco smiled weakly. First she had to betray her best friend and dance with Ruby. Then she had to audition for Brigham Powell. And now she had to do it wearing the trashiest outfit in Beverly Hills?

Then, remembering that everything she did was being photographed, Coco smiled a huge fake grin. It was like waiting for her own '80s-themed funeral.

CHAPTER
nineteen

mac

◀ Thursday   September 3 ▶

5 PM   SC brainstorming (put temporary
       Pinkberry high to use!)

7 PM   Work on project M.E.S.S. (Make Emily
       Skyler a Star!)

Mac sat on her pale green Louis XIV sofa chair, listening to the *Les Misérables* soundtrack and reexamining her social chair campaign on her glowing iBook. She slammed her computer shut with a snap on the slide show picture of Haylee Parda's victorious, social-chair-winning face. She felt *très, très* alone.

What was bugging Mac most was what Kimmie had said about auditions for *Deal with It* being closed. Kimmie was a gossip, but she wasn't a *liar*. If auditions were closed, then Mac needed to come up with a backup plan, or face the non-inspirational *Les Misérables* music and give up now. Not knowing if Emily could still try out for the part was driving her crazy. But there was one way to end her misery.

One very dishonest way.

In fact, it was probably illegal. But Mac was desperate.

She put on her favorite orange Tory Burch flats, left her bedroom, and padded down the carpeted hallway, making her way down the grand front stairs. She peered out an arched window and saw Jenner on the lawn practicing his volleyball serve as the sun set over the canyon. Her dad and Maude were playing water basketball in the pool. With her mother in New Zealand on the movie set, all Armstrongs were accounted for.

No one would know a thing.

She slipped into her mother's office on the first floor, closing the door gently behind her. Very gingerly, Mac tiptoed toward the glass-topped desk and set her trembling fingers on the keyboard. She typed her mother's password: *alphamom.*

Make that her ex-password.

Merde.

"Mac?"

Mac was so startled to see Erin standing in the doorway, she almost didn't notice her hideous green-and-orange thrift-store dress. Mac's heart raced as she decided what to do next.

"E-dawg! I was looking for you!" Mac said then, smiling as she stood up from behind the desk.

"Oh?" Erin put her hands on her hips. The green-and-orange fabric swirled around her ankles, expanding outward like an accordion.

"Yes. Remember that deal we made about my mom coming to your shows?"

"Yeah?" Erin said cautiously. She looked around, as if Adrienne Little-Armstrong might have the office bugged. It wasn't impossible.

Mac lowered her voice. "Well, actually, Erin, it's a two-part deal."

"What?" The color drained from Erin's face. "Mac . . ." she said nervously.

"All you have to do is tell me my mom's password. She changed it and I—"

"No no no no no no!" Erin cried, covering her ears like a child. "I can't hear a thing you're saying!"

Mac waited until Erin's fake temper tantrum was over. "Erin, I need your help more than ever." The quiver in her voice was real.

Erin looked around the room, apparently still checking for bugs, and mouthed, "Follow me." She led Mac through the French doors to the back lawn that overlooked Mulholland Drive, to a small patch of bright green grass far away from Lanyard, Maude, and Jenner.

"Mac, I haven't been sleeping at night. What I did at Urth Café was wrong. I could get fired. I should *never* have done that. Please understand."

Mac gave Erin her best glare. Usually she could scare Erin into doing whatever she wanted.

Jenner ran toward them, tossing his volleyball in the air. He was still wearing his board shorts from his afternoon surf session. "Dude, Erin, you gotta get me to the Billabong store. They just released this limited edition board I've been wanting for forever." He dangled the Prius keys in front of Erin's face. "Puhleeez!"

Although Jenner had a learner's permit, he still couldn't legally drive his brand-new black Audi A4 by himself until his sixteenth birthday, which was four months away.

Erin looked at Mac and then at Jenner. She took the keys from his hands.

"Er, we *gotta* go," Jenner said, too frantic to even make a stupid joke. "They close at eight." He brushed his white-blond hair off his face and stared at her expectantly.

"Good luck." Erin looked at Mac. "You've always been tops."

Mac watched in shock as Jenner and Erin pulled out of the driveway. Her negotiating skills had failed her.

With sweaty palms, she crept back into the study. She sat down in her mother's high-backed Aeron chair, not letting panic overtake her. What was the alpha mom's new password?

She looked around at the office. There was the snow globe from Paris her mom had almost chucked at the wall. The discarded *People* magazine was still in the recycling bin, where Mac had dropped it only two days ago. On the walls were her mother's framed diplomas from USC undergrad and Harvard Law, and on the shelf in front of them, displayed even more prominently, were her children's awards: Spelling Bee Champion for Maude. Winner, Huntington Beach Surf-Off '07, courtesy of Jenner. And then of course, her father's Oscar was being used as a bookend. The tiny golden man stared smugly at Mac. She shook her head. Everyone in her family was the best at something.

Suddenly Mac felt a sense of insta-calm, like when the air was so clear she could see the Hollywood sign from her bedroom. She typed in *numberone*.

Boom.

She opened her mother's Outlook e-mail program and typed *Davey Woodward*.

Boom again. There was an entire folder. She wasn't exactly sure what she was looking for, but like a good sale item at Barneys, she would know it when she saw it.

She scrolled quickly through e-mails, fueled by the giddy but very real fear of getting caught. She'd be grounded for all of eighth grade, possibly high school, if her mother ever found out what she was doing.

This was top-secret money information, stuff that maybe even the assistants didn't know.

Davey Woodward made $800,000 an episode?

Davey Woodward had his own assistant?

And then Mac struck gold:

To: alittlearmstrong@initiativeagency.com
Cc: alittlearmstrong_assistant@initiativeagency.com
alittlearmstrong_assistant2@initiativeagency.com
From: Holly.Wooker@CastingGirls.com
Subject: DEAL WITH IT Auditions

Adrienne,

Per our conversation today, please do keep us in mind if you think of a girl with the chops for DEAL WITH IT. Producers want to lock it up this weekend. Oh, and let's do lunch at Il Pastaio next week. Miss you, doll.

xoxo, Hol

Mac's heart thumped against her gold, initialed locket. In fact, her heart hadn't beaten that quickly since she was thirty seconds away from being the top bidder for vintage YSL lace-up heels on eBay. This was *a coup*.

The role was still totally up for grabs.

Just then, her phone blared its Pussycat Dolls ring, shattering her reverie. Coco's face smiled up at her, but Mac didn't have time to split her focus. She cringed, knowing that she'd ignored Coco's calls way too many times in one week. But this was for the greater good.

She needed to call Holly Wooker.

Mac reminded herself of one of her mother's power principles: *Act as if you own it.* Of course, Mac was taking it completely out of context to suit her purpose. But there was probably some power rule about taking things out of context, too.

Mac pulled the sleek black V-tech phone toward her. She knew business phone calls were fast and to the point. And she'd heard Charlotte call for auditions for her mother's clients a thousand times. It would be just like that time she went to art camp in Paris and told all the French girls that American kissing was totally different from French kissing. The secret to lying, she reminded herself, was to *treat it like a game*.

But as she picked up her mother's office phone, she could hear her mother's credo about honesty buzzing in her head: *We live in a dishonest world, which is why we have to be honest with each other.*

Oh well.

She took a sip of her mom's Fiji water and dialed the number to Holly Wooker Casting.

"Casting," the voice said after just one ring. It was too young to be Holly. Definitely an assistant.

Mac flipped through a *Vanity Fair* to keep herself relaxed.

"Hey this is . . . Jen," Mac said. "I'm filling in for Charlotte over at Initiative."

"But . . . I just talked to Charlotte?" the assistant said.

Double *merde*.

Mac's pulse revved and she twirled her Mintee bracelet several times for good luck. "Um, I'm new. She's training me," Mac explained. Before the conversation could get drowned in logistics, Mac said, "I'm supposed to tell you we have a girl for *Deal with It*."

"Holly is gonna love you for this," the assistant said excitedly.

Mac turned the phone away from her face so the assistant wouldn't hear her relieved exhale.

"She's phenomenal, she's new, she's fresh from the Midwest," Mac pitched, channeling her inner Adrienne. "Emily Skyler. Adrienne knows you're going to love her." Mac raked sand in her mother's Japanese garden, the same one that sat on her desk at Initiative. Apparently Mama Armstrong needed to stay calm at work, too.

"Oooohwonderful," the assistant cooed. "Do you have headshots?"

"We're still waiting for them to come in," Mac said, fake-sadly, hoping she wouldn't press the issue.

To her great relief, the girl replied, "We've only got tomorrow at 6 p.m. I know it's short notice, but they really want to move on this. Because we trust Adrienne, she'll go right to producers."

Normally actors had to audition several times before they were brought to see producers, who made the final decisions, because their time was too valuable to waste with people who weren't serious contenders.

"Friday. Perfect," Mac said, fluffing her hair. Mid-fluff, she remembered a very important detail. "Oh, by the way, Adrienne wants me to give you her temporary cell phone number. Her BlackBerry is being upgraded. She requests that you call her on that?"

"Hit me," the assistant said, and Mac spelled out her own cell phone number for the girl.

"We'll send you details," the girl said. "What's your e-mail address?"

"Just send it to Adrienne directly," Mac said. "My Initiative e-mail isn't set up yet."

"Okay. I'm hitting send as we speak," the girl said. "To Adrienne. Oooh, I never get to e-mail Adrienne. I feel special."

Mac felt special, too, that she was related to someone people were excited to e-mail. She watched the confirmation from Holly Wooker Casting pop into her mother's inbox.

"You're all set," the assistant said.

Click.

Mac opened her Louis Vuitton iPhone holder and jotted down the details of the audition as fast as she could. Then she deleted the e-mail and emptied the Outlook trash before her mother could possibly have a chance to glance down at her BlackBerry.

Mac looked down at her iPhone and smiled at the address. It represented her hard work and her social mojo, and the reason why she, Mac Little-Armstrong, was destined to be social chair.

She sauntered outside, where the setting sun cast a warm orange glow over the pool and yard, to treat herself to some French *Marie Claire* reading in her poolside hammock. She imagined discussing her social chair position at a family dinner right after Jenner mentioned an upcoming surf campaign and right before Maude talked about her recent chess win.

Everything felt right. She snapped a photo of herself just to savor the moment.

TWENTY

Emily's L.A. Itinerary

Friday, September 4

11 AM   Meet Mac for pre-audition something
        (brunch?)

6 PM   Audition for *Deal with It*. (Eek!)

8 PM   Kimmie Tachman's par-tay
        (true Hollywood party)

Friday morning at the Econo Lodge, Emily threw her new gold-flecked Splendid tee over her head and shimmied into her new wide-legged Paige jeans. Mac had bought her some basics on their way out of Fred Segal so she could "look L.A.-hot," which, apparently, was the best kind of hot. Emily practically floated into the clothes, she was so excited.

Mac was taking her "somewhere special" before her big audition, and Emily secretly hoped it would be a trendy L.A. brunch spot. She knew that Mac and her friends had brunch often, and that wasn't something she did back in Iowa. Plus, it was the night of Kimmie Tachman's Sweet Thirteen. Mac and Emily were going to race from the producers' office in Culver City down to Beverly Hills. Two A-list events in one night!

"Here I come, Hollywood," Emily quietly joked to herself in the mirror.

Emily's mom was in the shower, and Paige was still sleeping. Emily wanted to sneak out of the room before Paige could see her. Her outfit was definitely not something they'd sewn themselves, and Emily was clearly breaking their DLT (dress-like-twins) pact.

"Where did you get those clothes?" Paige's head popped up in bed behind her. She took out her retainer and moved it over by the digital clock.

"Oh, I just grabbed them when I was out 'cause I spilled stuff on my dress," Emily said, hoping Paige wouldn't press the issue. What she couldn't tell Paige was that there was a $2,040 stash of Mac-bought clothes under the Econo Lodge bed, stuffed behind the spare pillow.

"Why not just wear another dress?" Paige asked, smoothing down her frizzy hair. "I like our blue one with the red hearts."

"Oh yeah . . . I just don't have time to change," Emily lied, pulling her hair into a bun high atop her head.

"I'm confused." Paige uncrossed her arms and pulled the sheets over her lap. "Are you going out?"

"Didn't I tell you?" Emily asked, knowing full

well she hadn't told Paige anything. Emily swooped her eyelashes with Shu Uemura mascara.

"You wear makeup now?" Paige whispered.

Emily faced her best friend. She sat on the bed. "Paigie, I'm so sorry, but I have to go meet Mac and her mom before the audition today," Emily lied again. It seemed less like she was ditching her friend if a parent was supposedly there. "They say it's important."

"That's good." Paige nodded. She seemed happy to be talking about acting. "Adrienne Little-Armstrong knows what she's doing."

"Are you *sure* you don't mind if I go?" Emily asked, even though she'd already decided.

"Of course not," Paige said. "Lori and I will have a blast at the tar pits!"

"Oh God, I'm sorry." Emily said, just grateful that Paige was being so easygoing about all this. A part of her knew she should just invite Paige along, but Mac didn't seem interested in having other people around. And—even though Emily hated thinking this—it *was* easier without Paige.

"Besides, I'll still see you at Fred Segal at four, right?" Paige asked, standing up to stretch. "I'll meet you in front. I'll be the girl *freaking out*!"

Emily had forgotten they'd ever made those

plans. How was she going to make it to brunch, her audition, Kimmie's party, *and* Fred Segal?

Her phone buzzed. Mac was texting her.

"Oh no, Emily! What happened to your bracelet?" Paige asked, spotting Emily's bare wrist.

Emily pretended to be shocked. "Oh no!" she said, halfheartedly looking around the room. "It must have fallen off in bed." Actually, it was buried in the bottom of her LeSportsac duffel, where she'd stuffed it after her shopping spree. She would have plenty of time to wear a BFF bracelet when she got back to Iowa.

If she went back to Iowa.

"Don't worry, it couldn't have gone anywhere far." Paige smiled encouragingly.

Emily gulped. "Mac's outside. Gotta run. Luvya, babe!" she said, skipping out the door.

Erin drove Emily and Mac down Melrose to Elixir, which was hidden behind bamboo trees. "This is a tea bar," Mac said, as they entered the wood-paneled cottage. "Sometimes I do homework here. Gwyneth comes here when she's in L.A." She offered the last bit of information as though she were revealing something important, like the cure for cancer.

Emily scanned the blackboard menu above the

counter. She'd never been to a place that served just tea. It seemed very sophisticated and yet . . . boring. She secretly hoped Becks and Coco would show up and they'd all go get pancakes.

"So, are you having fun in L.A.?" Mac asked. Emily realized it was the first time they'd ever had a moment of girl talk.

"Yeah," Emily said slowly. "Yesterday we—"

"You know what?" Mac said, cutting her off. "This new look is really working for you. Let's get some elixirs and grab some shade."

Emily sighed. So much for girl talk.

They grabbed their five-dollar Mind over Muddle tonics and found some empty wooden benches under the bamboo trees. Mac put a napkin on the bench so she wouldn't get dirt on her bright-white Stella McCartney pants.

"Voilà!" Mac presented a script to Emily like it was a glass slipper once she'd sat down. "I stayed up until 2 a.m. highlighting your lines." It was in a red paper cover with the Initiative logo, with notes scrawled in the margin of almost every page.

"This must have taken you forever!" Emily said.

Mac shrugged inside her white off-the-shoulder prairie top. "It's what any good agent would do. I brought you here today so we could run lines."

Emily smiled. It wasn't brunch. It was *better*. It was something real actresses did. And with every day that passed, Emily was starting to think she could become a real actress, not just a girl who wanted to meet her star crush.

Although she wanted that, too.

"So, Mac, you think I'll be ready to meet Davey soon?" she asked a little tentatively, feeling her rosy cheeks turn rosier.

"Sooner than you might think." Mac wrinkled her freckled ski-slope nose and smiled.

For the next two hours, Emily read her lines as Mac turned the pages and played all the other parts. They went through the entire script. Emily thought she did a good job of acting like a boy. She lowered her voice and spoke without inflection.

When they finished, Mac twirled one of her wooden bracelets around her tan wrist.

Emily was getting to know Mac well enough to know that she only turned her bracelets when she was nervous about something. A painful truth might be on the way. She pressed her lips together to brace herself.

"Um, you do know that it's called *acting*, right?" Mac said.

"Um, yes?"

"'Cause what you're doing is *saying words*."

"Okay, so tell me how to act," Emily said, a little defensively.

"You're not a trained monkey," Mac said. "You're an *actor*. You're supposed to bring *your* choices to the material."

Emily chipped at her Leave It to Diva red nail polish from yesterday's makeover.

"Look, it's your first time doing this. But for example, in that scene where you convince the headmaster to let you stay at school, you need to tap into that place you were in when you pretended to be Corey Woodward at that party. Remember how badly you wanted in? Well, that's how badly Alex wants boarding school. She's from a boring Midwestern town. She wants out—she's destined for bigger things. I think you can relate to that, right?"

Just then Mac's phone rang. She looked down at the picture of Becks's smiling face. Mac turned the phone upside down and then looked back at Emily. "Never let your attention be diverted when you're with a client," she said, more to herself than to Emily. Emily smiled, feeling like she was as special to Mac as Becks, even if it was just for an hour or two.

"Can I try again?" Emily asked, plopping her empty glass on the table.

"I don't have to be anywhere until your audition," Mac said. "I've got all day."

With Mac's added insight, Emily ran the lines with Mac for another two hours. This time, when she finished, Mac smiled a genuine smile.

"Well-played, Emily Skyler, well-played," Mac said.

Emily grinned. "You know—" she started, and then looked down at her hands in her lap. Between the manicure and the jeans, she hardly looked like herself. But she *felt* like herself. "You're good at this," Emily said to Mac. "You really understand people."

"You think?" Mac said, looking down at the table. *Was Mac Little-Armstrong blushing?* "I like it," Mac said, as though realizing it for the first time.

For a second, Emily thought she saw a vulnerable side of Mac. But then, faster than a celebrity engagement, it vanished. Emily realized it must be lonely being Mac.

"Well, we should get moving," Mac said. "Your audition's in a little more than an hour."

Emily looked down at her blue swatch. It was 4:22. "I was supposed to meet Paige at Fred Segal twenty minutes ago!"

Mac shrugged. "She'll understand."

"But I promised her I'd be there," Emily said, reaching for her BFF bracelet, and then remembering it was gone. "I didn't realize this would take so long."

"When you become a star, you two can go shopping 24/7," Mac said easily. "Fred Segal will be sending *you* stuff. "

"It's just that—"

"Just call her," Mac instructed, braiding her long blond hair over her shoulder.

Emily swallowed and dialed the number, thinking that Paige had been doing a lot of understanding this week. Paige picked up on the first ring.

"Hey." Emily gritted her teeth and closed her eyes as if that would make the call a little easier.

"Hey! I'm in front of Fred Segal but I'm not peeking until you get here," Paige said.

Emily winced. "Yeah . . . about that . . ." Emily couldn't bring herself to say it.

"You *are* still meeting me here, right?" Paige asked. "That was our deal."

"It's just that—" Emily began.

"So you're ditching me?" Paige cut in, hurt and anger rising in her voice.

"I'm so sorry, but everything took a little longer than I thought it would," Emily said. She played with the straw of her empty drink. Her red fingernails looked a little menacing now.

Silence.

"Do what you need to do," Paige said finally. "Your mom and I will watch TV."

Click.

"Don't worry about her," Mac said, securing her braid with a ponytail holder as Emily set down her phone. "She'll get over it. Besides you need to start building relationships with people who matter."

Versus people who didn't matter?

Emily nodded, though she couldn't help but picture Paige standing in front of Fred Segal all alone, waiting for the one person who was supposed to treat her like she mattered, too. Wasn't that what best friends were for?

CHaPter
TWenTY-one

COCO

◀ Friday   September 4 ▶

10:15 AM   Rehearse on own (practice dancing in costume without flashing anyone, i.e., Brigham Powell)

11 AM   Rehearse with, um, partner

8 PM   Kimmie's Sweet Thirteen!

Coco stood in her Kelly Wearstler–designed pastel-green bedroom holding Madonna so that they were face-to-face.

"Ruby and I are getting better, aren't we, Madge?" Coco asked.

Madonna whimpered, her droopy eyes focused on Coco.

"That's a yes," Ruby said from where she was stretching on the carpet with a playful laugh.

Coco and Ruby had been practicing all morning in Coco's private dance studio, and now they were taking a ten-minute stretch break. The idea of having Ruby there no longer made Coco's head spin. She was used to Ruby enough that she wasn't crash-landing every time they practiced together. In fact, Coco was pretty sure they were getting better, even if they didn't have the dance down completely yet.

Coco was wearing a gold American Apparel tank top that left half of her naturally honey-tan stomach exposed. It was the closest she ever came to dressing wild and crazy. She rubbed her gold Macedonian sun necklace, a gift from her dad from his Athens hotel. It was supposed to bring her good luck, and she needed all the good luck she could summon. Madge had a matching dog tag, and Coco rubbed it for an extra dose.

She closed the doors to her wall-to-wall closet, so that full-length mirrors were visible across one wall of her room. She put the dog down, and Madonna immediately bounded over to where Ruby was stretching on the green-and-white carpet, licking her ballet flats.

"Why, hello, Madonna," Ruby said, scratching Madge's ears as though it were totally normal for her to be playing with Coco's dog. "Stretch time's over. Let's bang this out!" Ruby said, standing up and clapping her hands. She smiled like it was no big deal to learn a brand-new dance before a life-changing audition. Her attitude seemed to say, *Of course we will get this.*

Ruby followed Coco into the adjoining dance studio, her every muscle aching. Coco hit play on her sound system, and her own breathy voice filled the room.

This time, when the music started, Coco forgot about how bad she felt, and only focused on one thing: her dancing. Not her stiff joints, not her aching body, not Ruby, not the ugly outfits, not the audition. She just let her mind focus, step by step, on her routine. When the last bar of the music ended, they were still so in synch, their lips curled into smiles at the exact same time.

Finally, they'd nailed the routine.

"We did it! I knew we could!" Ruby said.

"We *did*!" Coco said, more surprised that *she* had done it, since Ruby's dancing was already amazing.

In a moment of giddiness, Coco ran over and embraced Ruby. They actually jumped up and down, hugging and squealing. And in that moment, Coco forgot she hated Ruby. She even forgot why she was supposed to.

When they pulled apart, Ruby's violet eyes lit up. She ran over to her pink American Apparel duffel bag and pulled out gigantic blue Bliss Spa bags.

"As much as I, um, appreciated your mom's outfit choices," Ruby began, "I just didn't think they were *us*. And so Elsa Winters was over at my house because she's consulting on my dad's next movie, and I asked her if she had any ideas . . ."

Elsa Winters was the editor in chief of *Look,* and

she was one of the most powerful women in fashion. Coco blinked twice, wondering what in the world would be in those bags.

"And this is what she threw together."

Coco peered into her baby-blue bag.

There were a black short-sleeved turtleneck, cropped black leggings under a short black pencil skirt, and white socks with black ballet slippers.

The outfit was very Audrey Hepburn, *Funny Face* chic.

And it was *gorgeous*.

"Love, love, love!" Coco cried, bounding toward Ruby to hug her one more time.

Then, realizing she was having *another* moment with Ruby, Coco pulled away.

"Back to work," she said. "Let's take it from the top."

She had the biggest audition of her life in twenty-four hours. She couldn't let anything distract her. Not herself. Not Mac.

And certainly not a nice gesture from Ruby Goldman.

chapter
TWENTY-TWO

becks

◀ Friday   September 4 ▶

2 PM Whole Foods w/ dad

5 PM Get ready for Kimmie's (allow time for snafus)

8 PM Par-tay!

B ecks stood in her bedroom, trying to remember how to sparkle her eyelids the way Salome had done for Emily at Frédéric Fekkai. It wasn't working. Neither was the concealer she'd attempted to put on, which was caked around her nostrils and in the crevices of her eyes like putty-colored eye-goobers. Becks took a deep breath and turned away from the mirror, glad she'd given herself a few hours to get ready. Her lip had mostly de-swelled from yesterday, but she didn't want any more disasters.

Becks glanced at the straightening iron on her dresser, a gift from Mac: Its red ON light was like a stoplight.

Maybe that should have been a sign.

She lowered herself onto her water bed and glanced around the room. The walls were painted in gradients of blue, starting with a pale blue ceiling, which got darker down the wall, eventually blending into an inky blue-black near the floor. It made Becks feel like she lived at the bottom of the Pacific. The rest of her room just looked like it had fallen victim to a Malibu earthquake. The dresser was a jumbled mess of colorful makeup compacts, blushes, bronzers, and hair sprays. Jewelry spilled out of the Little Mermaid jewelry box she'd had since first grade. A scary mass of dresses tumbled out of the closet. She was the only one who hadn't bought a new dress at Fred Segal, since Mac had strongly dissuaded—i.e., forbade—her from buying the one that didn't pass the arms-lifted test.

Becks picked up her iPhone and speed-dialed Mac. She needed fashion advice, stat.

"Make it fast, babe. I'm in a meeting," Mac answered.

"I just . . . I don't know how to get ready for tonight," Becks began. "I don't even have a dress picked out and I—"

"Okay, here's the deal," Mac said quickly, drawing in a breath. "For makeup, all you need is Nars coral lip gloss, which I'll bring for you. Just brush your hair with a left-side part, and spray it down with the finisher I got you at Frédéric Fekkai, two pumps per side. Wear the low-backed Versace I picked out for you in the spring, the cream-colored one. It'll look perfect with your tan."

"Thanks, Mac." Becks breathed a sigh of relief.

"Oh, and one last thing—don't use bronzer, and don't go in the sun: It'll throw off the color contrast. That means no surfing, okay? Good. *Ciao bella*. Luv you!" Mac said, and hung up the phone.

Click.

Becks lay back on her water bed and turned her head to face the enormous picture window. Out on the beach, Austin was throwing a stick for Boone to fetch. She sat up and moved toward the window. It was a gorgeous late afternoon, and the waves were enormous—even from here you could see the white crests. And it wasn't like it was going to take her long to get ready now that she knew exactly what to do.

She threw on her Quiksilver hula-print bikini, tied it tight, and bounded out the door, grabbing SPF 30 sunscreen as she went.

What Mac didn't know wouldn't hurt her . . .

Outside the wind whipped through her hair and the sand felt warm under her feet.

"Look who's here!" Austin said to Boone when he spotted Becks, breaking into a big smile. "Can you say hi to Becks?" Boone barked enthusiastically and Becks giggled.

"I thought you had your fancy-schmancy party tonight," Austin teased.

"I do, but a girl's gotta surf." Becks shrugged. She squirted a blob of Coppertone into her hands and slathered it all over her arms. When she'd covered every conceivable inch, not forgetting her toes, she reached around to do her back. She twisted her long arms, trying to reach the middle.

Austin laughed as he watched her contort herself. "You look like a circus freak," he noted, and Boone barked in agreement. "Need a hand?"

Becks froze. The very idea of Austin touching her made her blush uncontrollably. She turned away from him so he wouldn't see her red-hot cheeks.

"Sure. Thanks," she said casually, holding the tube out behind her, still turned away from him. "I'm giving you a *very* important task," Becks joked. "Mac will murder me if I change my tan level."

"I'll do my best," Austin said. "Wouldn't want to upset the leader of the *ick*!"

Becks held her hair up in a bun and waited, holding her breath. And then, starting with the top of her neck, Austin made lines all the way down and across her back. He seemed to be going pretty slowly, but she didn't mind one bit. The sunscreen was cold but his fingers were warm, and her whole body felt like it was tingling. Becks wished she had a long torso, like Mac sometimes said about girls who shouldn't wear low-rise jeans, just so he'd have to touch her for a little bit longer.

"Okay, done," Austin pronounced, after what felt like a warm and wonderful eternity.

They grabbed their boards and surfed until the sky turned dusty pink. When the sun had almost set, Becks dragged herself out of the water. She'd have just enough time to shower and make it to the party if she went at turbo speed.

She knew she should be excited about the party, and worried about getting ready in time, but all Becks could think about was how wonderful it had felt when Austin's hands were on her back. She made a mental note to buy lots and lots of sunscreen.

CHapter
TWenTY-THRee

Emily's L.A. Itinerary

Friday, September 4

6 PM AUDITION, OHMYGOSH, OHMYGOSH,
         OHMYGOSH

"**F**ocus, babe!" Mac said, snapping her fingers in front of Emily's face. Her wooden bracelets clunked down her elbows. "When you walk into that room, you want to project sweetness. But just be yourself: Everyone's going to pick up on your vibe."

Emily didn't bother to ask how you could pick up on a vibe. She just hoped her right leg wouldn't tremble and make her look like a freak. Erin had dropped them off exactly thirty minutes early for the audition, and they were sitting in the Executive Bungalow on white Philippe Starck benches in front of suite 202.

Emily was dressed in the same baseball cap/ polo shirt/cargo pants combo she'd worn at Abercrombie when she'd acted her way into the boys' changing room, which Mac had said would be good luck. Thankfully the clothes seemed like they'd been washed since their last outing, and now smelled Downy-fresh. Since they were the last audition of the day, they had the waiting room all to themselves, and it was so quiet Emily worried Mac would be able to hear her grinding her teeth.

From the enormous second-floor window they could look out onto the whole studio. It was like being in another world. There were sets of New York City streets, a sign for *Jeopardy!* studios, and white bungalows with green shutters that reminded her of the Los Angeles from old black-and-white movies. Fresh-out-of-college boys holding walkie-talkies cruised the fake New York in golf carts.

Finally, the door to suite 202 opened. "Emily Skyler, I'm Giselle. We'll see you now," said a supermodel-tall redhead with little or no inflection. Definitely not mean, but definitely not warm. She held the door open.

Emily walked calmly into suite 202, with Mac a few steps behind. The room was like a shrine to Zen minimalism: a bare wooden floor, white walls, white window panes, one white couch, and one Eames armchair behind a steel table. The only decoration was a lamp shaped like a revolver. A man and a woman sat on the white couch, and Emily recognized the famous auteur-director Shane Reed. He wore a very tight blue velvet suit and rectangular, thick-framed glasses. Next to him sat a severe-looking blond woman in a suit.

"Look at you, dollface!" Shane said, smiling at Emily. She couldn't believe that Shane Reed, the notoriously stormy director, was calling *her* doll-face. For a second, she wondered what to do; then she spotted Mac, sitting in the back of the room on a folding chair, and Emily remembered to stay sweet and smiley. She flashed Shane a toothy grin.

When Shane sat down, she realized that the man in the armchair next to him was Elliot Tachman.

E-Tach.

The same guy she'd watched accept dozens of Academy Awards. He had a scruffy beard and wild curly hair. But today instead of a tux, he wore jeans and a Michigan sweatshirt.

Emily pinched her thigh through the pockets of her baggy boy-jeans, just to be sure she wasn't dreaming.

She scanned the room and made eye contact, briefly, with everyone. On the other side of Shane was a woman in a pin-striped suit with long blond hair pulled into a ponytail. Behind them were seven assistant-looking people sitting on silver folding chairs. She tripled-checked the room to be absolutely sure that she hadn't missed Davey. He definitely wasn't there.

She sighed. Another time. Besides, it was probably a good thing, since Davey would only make her more nervous. And if she got the part, well, she'd have to meet him when they were filming, right?

"I'm Anne Rupert," the woman in the suit announced in a smoker's voice, resting her elbows on the steel table. She wore an enormous glinting diamond ring on her wedding finger. "I'm Shane's producing partner. We're going to have you stand over there, in the center." She gestured toward two pieces of duct tape that made an X on the floor.

Emily walked to where she had been directed, feeling a dozen strangers' eyes on her. She imagined she was a pirate following a treasure map to keep herself from getting nervous. Emily hadn't realized that an audition would be a performance, beginning the second she stepped into the room. As she stood on the X, wondering what they were going to have her do next, the door opened, and all heads turned to see the late arrival.

There, framed in the doorway, stood *Davey Farris Woodward.*

He casually glanced around suite 202, a cocky

half-smile on his tan face. He looked like he always did on *Just the Five of Us*, his black hair wavy, a dimple in his chin. But in real life, his features were sharper, and his skin glowed even more. He was holding a Coffee Bean Ice Blended and wearing Diesel jeans. Emily couldn't stop looking at him.

Apparently nobody else could either. All the assistants—even Shane—followed him with their eyes as he sauntered over to the couch. The only people who seemed immune to the DFW Spell were Mac, who was staring only at Emily, and Elliot Tachman, whose eyes were focused on his Black-Berry.

"Davey, my man!" Shane said, standing up to greet the star.

"Shane-dawg!" Davey said, patting him on the back as they shook hands. "Good to see ya."

The assistants were still staring openmouthed at Davey. Then Emily realized their gaze had shifted toward *her*. Because Davey was headed her way. He gave her a small nod and then stood a few feet away from her, facing the producers' table. Emily stared straight ahead, focusing on Anne Rupert's wedding ring and trying not to imagine her own fantasy wedding to Davey.

"Listen up, dollface," Shane said, waving a Whole

Foods takeout container. He was surprisingly tall and fit. "We're going to have you do the climactic scene," he said, stabbing what appeared to be seaweed salad with a clear plastic fork. "GISELLE!" he screeched. "Where are my vitamins?" The redhead returned with a clear baggie of six rainbow-colored pills and a glass of milky water.

"What is this?" Shane barked.

"Coconut water, per your request," she said.

"I DON'T DO ADDITIVES!"

"This is the brand you approved."

"Oh. Right," he said, throwing his head back and chugging the additive-free coconut water.

Emily wondered how he'd react if he didn't like her audition. But then she noticed Davey smiling at her. She smiled back at her crush, shyly. Her leg instantly started to tremble.

Shane took one last swig of his coconut water and slammed the glass on the steel table. Then, like a lion after the kill, he wiped his mouth and looked at them. "You've read the script, right, dollface?"

Emily nodded.

"Good," Shane smiled. "You probably learned your lines, studied your character, all that jazz, right?"

Emily nodded again.

"That's great!" Shane said, pausing to take a bite. "Because I want you to forget everything you prepared. Throw it out the window. We're going to improvise. Just make it all up!" He tossed his hands up in the air like he was throwing confetti. "Im-pro-vise, fun, fun, fun."

Emily stared at him blankly. Improvise? She had no idea how to do that.

"Here's the deal with me and scripts," Shane said, picking up the red cover of *Deal with It* from the table. "I can take 'em or leave 'em," he said. "We know the story: Boy meets girl, boy loses girl, blah, blah, blah, I'm bored." He dropped the script back on the table.

Emily put her hand on her boy-jeaned leg to stop the shaking. Why hadn't Mac warned her that he was crazy? She looked back at Mac, who pointed at her own toothy grin, reminding Emily to smile. Emily froze her face into a half-grimace that was all teeth.

"I can watch you say your lines till the cows come home—and by the way, the cows are *not* coming home—but what I won't know is if there's *chemistry*," he said, still staring at Emily. A piece of seaweed salad flew from his mouth, but he kept talking. "It's all about chemistry. You get it, right, dollface?"

Emily nodded for the millionth time, not knowing what she was supposed to say or if she was even supposed to speak. She hoped Davey wasn't wondering why he was auditioning opposite a deaf-mute. She couldn't bring herself to look at him.

"So why don't you two do the last scene of the movie? Just make it up, I don't care." He waved his hands at them. "Davey's a great improviser. Just have fun."

Davey turned to Emily. "You know the ending, right?" His voice was deep and soft at the same time.

Emily nodded. Her mind was racing like she'd downed four cans of Tab. At the end of the script, she was supposed to reveal that she was a girl and kiss Davey. Emily had never kissed a boy. She'd barely practiced on her pillow, let alone *tried it out on a movie star*. She hadn't even gotten to kiss that wax statue of Davey.

"Don't worry," Davey whispered, like it was no big deal. "We'll have fun." His melodic voice might have calmed down another girl, but it made Emily so nervous she felt like she was going to topple over. She leaned in toward Davey to say "Thanks," but hadn't realized his face was so close.

She head-butted him.

"OW!" They both said at the same time, each holding their heads.

"You really know how to put a guy in his place," Davey joked, rubbing his nose. Shane laughed, and the others followed suit.

Just as Emily was about to panic, she spotted Mac smiling, as though this were all part of the plan. "That's how I roll," she said easily.

The room erupted in laughter again. *So I guess this is improvising?*

"Seriously, I'm sorry!" Emily whispered to Davey.

"Don't even worry about it," Davey said, taking his hand off his face. "Just be careful with that kiss." He winked again.

"So should we get started?" Davey asked the room.

Everyone nodded.

Emily took a deep breath. Even if they were just improvising, she was going to have to tap into her character. She paused, and shuffled her feet just like she had that day at the Grove. She swung her shoulders low and tilted the hat down so that it covered most of her face. And then she felt that familiar *click*. It was as though the audience of Hollywood people vanished, and once again, Emily was Jeff, totally alone in the room with Davey. She was so absorbed in acting that she actually stopped thinking about what it would be like to kiss Davey. But not totally. Because for this role she wasn't really Jeff; she was a girl *pretending* to be Jeff, a girl who was both desperate to stay in character and to break out of it.

"So there's something I have to tell you," Emily said with the deep, from-her-gut voice that she'd used for Jeff.

"Whatsup?" Davey said. His reaction was so natural it was hard to tell if he was acting or not.

"It's hard to explain," she said slowly, shoving her hands in the pockets of her baggy jeans.

"Dude, just say it," Davey said, half impatiently, half nervously.

Emily looked at him for a moment, as a girl pretending to be someone she wasn't but wanting desperately for the boy she liked to see the real her. "Maybe I'll show you," Emily said in her normal voice. She took off her cap and let her cinnamon hair tumble down her face.

"You're a . . . girl?" Davey froze, too stunned to move.

Emily didn't think; she just reacted to Davey. "I'm sorry I couldn't tell you. I wanted to tell you," she said, letting the ache and longing filter into her voice. She leaned closer to him.

"I don't know what to say," Davey said, still not moving. You could practically see the thoughts racing across his character's face.

And then, without even thinking, Emily put her hands on Davey's shoulders. "You don't have to say anything," she said softly.

He leaned in . . . *slowly* . . . and their lips touched.

Her first kiss.

It was three Mississippis long, and when she leaned back, she let her hands rest on his shoulders an extra second before she let go. After they pulled apart, they stood staring at each other, both too stunned to say a word.

And then, snapping back to reality, Emily realized she had just touched lips with Davey Woodward. And she was in the middle of an audition. She suddenly noticed assistants were writing notes on their scripts and their clipboards. She wondered if they were making fun of her for being a dorky kisser. Had she kissed Davey wrong? All they did was brush lips . . . was that not how you did it? Did she seem stupid impersonating a guy? She didn't even have the energy to fake a smile. Her right leg was shaking so fast it was practically drumming the floor.

Just as Emily put her arm down to control her right leg, Shane stood up and clapped once. Then he paused, and clapped again. Then the other producers stood up, and began slowly clapping too. The assistants followed. Even Giselle.

"Ladies and gentlemen," Shane said, "I think we've found our girl."

Emily gasped. They liked her? Emily looked at Davey, but his BlackBerry rang from his pocket and he reached down to answer it. He gave her a quick smile, saluted the producers, and walked out the door, his phone to his ear.

Before Emily could follow him, Giselle walked over and put her arm around her. "Great job today," she said in a sweet voice, as if she'd believed in Emily all along. "We'll be in touch."

"Thank you," Emily said, truly meaning it. Mac grabbed Emily's hand and led her out the door. They were almost into the hallway when Giselle called after them.

"Oh, one last thing," she said in the toneless voice she'd used earlier. "You're with Initiative, right?"

Emily looked at Mac. She nodded slowly.

"And you're being repped by Adrienne Little-Armstrong?" Giselle asked. "'Cause the new assistant had no contact info for you when I called earlier today."

It was so quiet that she could hear the golf carts outside, whizzing across the lot.

"My mom's out of the country," Mac jumped in. "If you need anything, she'll be back in the office on Monday."

"No rush. I just wanted to make sure that Adrienne is the point person on Emily."

"Definitely," Mac said, nodding confidently.

Giselle rolled her eyes. "Assistants never know anything." She sighed. "You girls take care," she added sweetly as she closed the door to suite 202.

Emily smiled as she practically bounded down the hallway, hoping she might catch Davey on his way out. There was no sign of him, but Emily told herself she would just have to find him on their first day of shooting.

Erin was waiting for them in a parking spot just outside the building. As soon as Erin started the car, Mac screamed. Emily, who had so much pent-up energy, screamed, too.

Aaaaaaahhhhhhhhhhhhhhhhhhhhhhh!

"Ladies and gentlemen, I think we've found our girl," Mac said in a low, pretentious voice, imitating Shane. "Hello, new movie star Emily Skyler!" She slow-capped a few times and burst into giggles.

Emily giggled, too. "So I guess that went pretty well," she said with a grin.

"So well that I'm already thinking about the Hollywould shoes I'm going to buy with my first commission," Mac told her confidently.

But Emily barely heard. All she could think about was her next kiss with Davey.

CHAPTER
TWENTY-FOUR

mac

◀ Friday   September 4 ▶

8 PM   K-Tach's party

8:01 PM   Inner Circle's grand entrance (ICGE)

8:02 PM   Announce and celebrate Emily Skyler's stardom!

8:03 PM   Gloat about guaranteed social chair victory!

Mac and Emily hopped out of the Prius and into the driveway of the Regent Beverly Wilshire for Kimmie Tachman's party, just as Coco, driven by her butler, Pablo, pulled up in her CK-emblazoned Bentley. Mac and Emily had changed in the car, en route from the studio. As planned, Emily wore her gold-and-silver Cavalli disco dress, and Mac wore the micropleated aquamarine Tracy Reese from Fred Segal. Coco had on a plum-colored D&G one-strap minidress, and Mac knew Becks would be wearing the low-backed Versace as instructed.

Mac was so thrilled about Emily's audition, she couldn't even be upset that Becks had texted saying she'd be ten minutes late, hence ruining the ICGE. She looked from Emily, her budding star, to Coco, her forever friend. She stood in the middle and linked arms with both girls as they walked into the hotel.

Although Mac and Coco had been to several parties at the Regent Beverly Wilshire, a.k.a the *Pretty Woman* hotel, what they saw took their breath away. Elliot Tachman was notorious for going all out for his kids' parties, and Kimmie's Sweet Thirteen was no exception. The ballroom had been totally redecorated to look like the set of *The Lion King* on Broadway. The marble floor had been covered in sand, and there were rock outcroppings made of gray foam extending from the walls. The parquet dance floor had been painted blue to look like an oasis in the middle of the desert. Real cast members from the musical had been flown in from New York to perform during the cake-cutting ceremony. "Safari carts" picked up people who got tired of dancing.

Emily, Mac, and Coco went over to a large check-in table that was made to look like a mud-and-straw village hut. A woman dressed like a wild boar read names off a list.

"Mackenzie Little-Armstrong," Mac said.

The woman tapped the paper with her highlighter, then reached under the table and handed Mac a green feather boa and a souvenir backpack airbrushed with Kimmie's baby picture. The boa was actually sort of fun, but it clashed with her Tracy Reese. Mac handed it to Emily.

"Emily Mungler," Emily said.

The boar-lady with the highlighter looked down at her page. She scrolled up and down several times. "I'm sorry, I don't see your name."

"Maybe you're listed as Corey Woodward?" Mac teased. She turned to the boar-lady. "She's my plus-one."

"Mac!" a nasal-y voice called out. "Where's the guy from Abercrombie?" Kimmie asked, peering behind Emily and Coco to see if he was hiding behind them. She looked like she was ready to pounce.

Literally.

Kimmie was wearing a hot pink Jill Stuart mini-dress, and her frizzy hair was brushed into a wild mane. Her face was painted to look like that of a lion.

"Surprise!" Mac said, gesturing to Emily. "*He's* a *she*. We were rehearsing for *Deal with It*. And it paid off, 'cause she just got the part!"

"Ooooh, congratulations!" Kimmie said, flicking her pin-on lion tail. "Well, I have to say I thought you were a really cute guy, but I'm so glad you could be here, even if you're a girl." She made a paw with her hand. "Have a good time. Rrrrrrrrr."

Mac made a lazy, ironic paw back at Kimmie just as Becks bounded over, her strawberry-blond hair fluttering around her face.

"Excuse me, Mademoiselle Becks, where have you been?" Mac asked, pretending to check the time on her invisible watch.

"Sorry," Becks said, her cheeks coloring pink. "It, um, took me longer to get ready than I thought."

"Forgiven," Mac replied matter-of-factly. "It was worth it. You look great." Becks was wearing the ivory-colored dress with a teal pashmina. Sometimes Mac forgot how beautiful her tomboy friend was.

"Hurry and check in. We need to par-tay."

When Becks returned, the girls finally looked at their seating arrangements.

"Table six," Mac said, reading hers. She glanced around the ballroom for their table.

"Six," Coco repeated.

"Six," Becks added.

"Six-six-six, what a great omen," Mac offered dryly.

"More like Table Sucks," Coco noted, following Mac's gaze to the back of the ballroom. In the far corner, table six was barely visible in the dim light of the EMERGENCY EXIT sign. It was called the Hyena Table, and the centerpiece was a giant hyena, with hyena balloons floating up to the top. One of the rocky outcroppings stuck out of the wall above the table, threatening to fall at any moment.

"Is this a joke?" Mac asked, knowing that it

wasn't. Getting to their table would require a walk of shame past everyone, because everyone had a better table. In the center of the ballroom, Kimmie sat at the Pride Table, with cute lion cubs and balloons shaped like lion faces.

And Ruby Goldman sat at her side.

Mac bristled. How could Kimmie just shove them into a corner like that? The Inner Circle was supposed to be *in the center of things*. She decided it must have been a mistake, not a forecast for the year to come.

Before Mac could get too annoyed, the zebra-suited DJ started to play the Electric Slide. A slow smile spread across her face. "Um, question: What should we be doing right now?"

"Dancing!" Becks and Coco shouted in unison. Emily just sort of smiled and looked nervously around the ballroom.

Mac felt bad for Emily, who didn't know all their rituals. But the Electric Slide, as cheesy and retro as it was, was the Inner Circle's song. In sixth and seventh grade, they had all danced to it for the BAMS talent show, dressed as 1970s roller girls. She grabbed Emily's hand so she'd know she was welcome.

All four girls started to dance together, and as

they moved, Mac looked at her friends lovingly. Becks and Coco had been there for her since kindergarten, and Emily, in her stunning disco dress, moving around happily with a magnetic smile on her face, was starting to look like one of the group. The circle, Mac realized, was widening.

As she took a step back and to the side, Mac noticed Coco looking at her anxiously. Across the room, Ruby smiled at them with her shark teeth.

"Babe, I need to talk to you!" Coco said. "It's important."

"Tell me later!" Mac shouted over the music. She was on such a high, she didn't want anything to interrupt it. She stepped to the music with an almost-silly smile on her face. And then she started shaking her hips, not caring that she was supposed to be stepping forward or backward or to the side, just dancing happily. The other girls followed suit and started improvising, shimmying like crazy. Coco did a few steps from her dance routine, and Emily spun around in a circle. Becks took off her pashmina and threw it over Mac's head and around her waist, twisting it from side to side like they were tangoing.

There was a gasp from behind them, and Mac saw Ruby, in a green flapper-style dress and metallic green heels, point to Becks's back. "That's gotta hurt," Ruby commented to Ellie Parker, who stood beside her. Ellie giggled.

Mac looked at them in confusion.

"What are you talking about?" Becks asked, turning to face Ruby.

When she turned, her bare back faced Mac, and what Mac saw made her want to throw up: Becks was totally sunburned, and in the middle of her bright-pink back was a giant, pale *A*. Someone had deliberately formed that letter with strategically applied sunscreen. There was no way Becks could have or would have sun-tattooed herself. And not with an *A*.

Mac crossed her arms and glared at Becks.

"What?" Becks stammered.

"The evidence is on your back. I told you no surfing today. And you obvio didn't listen."

Becks's face turned as red as her back. "What? No, I—" she started to say.

Mac couldn't believe Becks was lying right to her face.

"If you're going to be social chair, a.k.a. control *all* of our social lives, it might be good to start by keeping tabs on your friends," Ruby cut in sarcastically. Mac had almost forgotten she was there.

The other Electric Sliders continued to dance around their small cluster, moving through the steps as they pretended to dance, but secretly watching the Ruby-Mac showdown.

"Thanks for your concern," Mac said fake-sweetly. "But my friends and I tell each other everything."

"Oh really," Ruby said, blinking her over-mascaraed eyelashes. Ruby's green feather boa matched her emerald green dress perfectly. Mac wondered if she'd known Kimmie's décor choices in advance and had planned her outfit around them. "Well then, Coco's probably told you about her new dance partner, right?"

"Some random girl," Mac replied without thinking. "See you later, Ruby." She turned back toward Becks to finish their conversation.

"You know, I've been called a lot of things," Ruby mused, twirling a lock of long blond hair around her finger, "but never *some random girl.*"

Mac knew from the look on her face that Ruby wasn't lying. *Ruby was Coco's dance partner?* Mac's eyes widened, looking back and forth from Coco to Ruby. And then it hit her, like back-to-back tidal waves, that Ruby's big project was auditioning for Brigham Powell . . . with *Coco.* Her best friend had known all along what Ruby was up to, and had kept it from Mac. Even worse, she was dancing with the enemy.

"I've been trying to tell you," Coco said help-lessly.

The final chords of the Electric Slide were wind-ing down, but nobody was dancing anymore. A small crowd had formed around the Inner Circle, Ruby and Ellie, whispering and pointing nervously, like a dance circle gone bad.

"I guess you didn't try hard enough," Mac snapped. There was nothing she hated more than being made a fool of. And yet here she was, with a crowd of people looking at her like she'd just attempted the Worm and smacked her teeth on the floor. The hyena balloons anchored on table six seemed to laugh at her.

"Hot off the presses!" Kimmie said, waltzing her way through the crowd to where Ruby, Coco, and Mac were exchanging stony glares. She waved her red NV phone in the air "Producers are going with Anastasia Caufield as the lead in *Deal with It*." Kimmie smiled, reading off the screen. "My dad's assistant texts me all the *Variety* headlines before they go to print 'cause he knows I love to know what's going on," she said. Then, spotting Emily, Kimmie covered her mouth. "Oh no. I'm sorry. Really. I just remembered you were—" She was too embarrassed to finish.

Ruby smiled gleefully. "Anastasia Caufield, huh?" she repeated, looking directly at Mac. "You may want to rethink your campaign slogan, Macadamia Nut."

For the first time, Mac had nothing to say. Her mouth opened and closed silently. Emily hadn't gotten the part. And she wasn't going to be social chair. Standing in the middle of the blue-painted dance floor, Mac felt like she was drowning.

Emily blinked twice and looked like she was fighting back tears. "Well, who wants to dress like a guy *all day long*?" Emily tried to laugh it off. "Besides, there's always next time, right, Mac?" She turned to look at Mac hopefully, her brown eyes wide.

"There is no next time," Mac said miserably. "It'll be too late next time."

"Too late for what?" Emily asked, confused.

"Did she not tell you?" Ruby turned to Emily, stroking her green feather boa like a pet snake. "Mac 'n' Cheese here was just going to use your success to win an election at our school," she said, smiling like a tiger watching its prey at the watering hole. "But really, who could blame her? She was trying to compete with *me*." She gave Mac a wink as she turned away on her metallic heel. "See you in school!" she cried as she made her way back to the Pride Table with Ellie and Kimmie in her wake.

The crowd around them started to disperse, leaving Mac, Emily, Coco, and Becks alone in the middle of the empty dance floor, like lions that had been rejected by the pride.

Emily bit her lip. "Oh." Her right leg was shaking. "Is that true?"

Mac didn't say anything. There was so much more to it, but the words wouldn't come. Instead, she said the only thing that came to mind: "How could you, Coco? You knew how much this meant to me!"

Coco's jaw dropped. "How much this meant to *you*?" she asked, incredulous. "I've been working toward this audition my whole life!"

Becks took a step closer to Mac, towering over her for the first time. "How about thinking a little less about social chair and a little more about your friends?"

"How about you brand your back with Austin's name, Becks," Mac shouted. "Oh, wait! You already did."

Emily took off her feather boa and rolled it into a ball. "Good luck with social chair, Mac."

"You know what, I'm out of here, too," Coco said.

"Me three." Becks, picked her blue pashmina up from the floor and draped it over her arm, not caring that the giant white *A* was still exposed on her back.

"You guys can't just leave!" Mac yelled. No one walked away from Mackenzie Little-Armstrong.

And with that, Mac stood all alone at an A-list party. She crept off the dance floor and out the door.

She had to. It was a matter of social survival.

chapter
TWENTY-FIVE

Emily & Paige's L.A. Itinerary

Saturday, September 5

8:15 AM	Wake up, decide outfit w/ Paige
9 AM	Econo Lodge breakfast (sugary cereal!)
10.30 AM	Fred Segal for vintage tees
1 PM	Lunch @ Subway (wearing new tees?)

"Can you even believe we're finally here?" Paige looked around Fred Segal as if she were inside a treasure chest. To girls like Emily and her best friend, the Tory Burch glittering tunics were like hidden gold.

Except Emily didn't care about this treasure anymore.

"I know, it's crazy!" Emily hoped she was faking her enthusiasm believably enough. She still hadn't been able to admit to Paige she'd already been to Fred Segal with Mac. It was one thing to run lines with someone; it was quite another to go *shopping*.

The girls were back to wearing matching outfits. Today's choice was yellow gingham dresses (sewn by Paige) and emerald green cardigans (American

Eagle). Emily had felt too guilty to tell Paige that she really was over the whole DLT thing. She'd already decided she'd go along with it for the rest of vacation out of guilt, but she made a note to herself: This *had* to stop when they got back to Iowa.

Paige walked around the store like it was Buckingham Palace, her brown eyes wide. She approached a rack of Free People jersey dresses and reached out to touch them, then pulled her hand back quickly as if they might bite.

Emily wondered if she'd looked this pathetically naïve when she first came here, then felt terrible for thinking that about her best friend. She touched her BFF bangle, which she'd unearthed from under the bed this morning, and reminded herself how lucky she was that she had a down-to-earth, real friend. "Real" being the key word.

"I can't believe you're not freaking out right now!" Paige said, finally working up the courage to pick up one of the jersey dresses. She looked at the price tag. "A hundred and eighty-five dollars! For cotton!"

Emily smiled weakly. "Yeah, that's a lot."

Emily's time in L.A. had been a dream-turned-nightmare. She couldn't believe she'd been stupid enough to believe she could become a movie star, and that Mackenzie Little-Armstrong had been try-ing to help her out of the goodness of her heart.

Paige reached for a black sequin Robert Rodri-guez dress. Mac would probably dismiss it as too look-at-me. She shook her mane of cinnamon-brown hair, trying to get Mac's voice out of her head.

Across the marble floor, Marianne, the salesgirl who'd been part of the Emily Skyler makeover, was folding Splendid and James Perse T-shirts on a velvet-lined table in the corner of the room. She wore another Diane von Furstenberg dress with clunky heels.

"Look! It's Reese Witherspoon!" Emily said, tilt-ing Paige's body so she faced the back of a blond woman by the jeans bar who was definitely *not* La Witherspoon.

"Where? You see Reese?" Paige asked incredu-lously, way too loud.

"That way!" Emily said, dragging Paige across the marble floors to the opposite end of the store. She lost sight of Marianne as they ducked behind a rack of Sanctuary khakis.

"Emily Skyler!" Marianne appeared from behind them, startling Emily, who stood reluctantly from the chair. She air-kissed Emily. "It's so good to see you again!"

Paige arched an eyebrow at her. *Again?*

"Uh, hi," Emily said, her right leg starting to bounce nervously. "Great to see you," she said, split ends–checking her long brown waves. "We're actually just getting going!" She made a motion toward the door, hoping Paige would follow.

"Are you happy with the dress? The Rock & Republic? And the C&C? What about the James Perse tunic?" Marianne asked sweetly.

Oh no.

"How much did you get *last time* you were here, Emily *Skyler*?" Paige snapped.

Marianne looked back and forth nervously between Emily and Paige. "I should go take care of some things," she stammered. "Let me know if you need anything. I'll just be over there," she said, walking backwards and almost knocking over a mannequin in a gold Materialust tee.

"Well, I feel like a big fat idiot," Paige said, crossing her arms.

"I'm sorry, I just—I needed some new clothes," Emily said lamely.

"What's wrong with our dresses?" Paige gasped.

"Nothing's *wrong* with our dresses," Emily examined a yellow Yaya jacket to avoid Paige's piercing eye contact. "It's just that they're not very L.A."

"Since when do you have to dress *L.A.*?" Paige asked, putting her hands on her hips.

"I just think we look a little stupid, okay?" Emily snapped. She regretted it the moment it left her mouth. But it was true: No other girls on the street were dressed the same, unless they were five and/or *actual* identical twins.

"Oh-kay," Paige said, staring right at Emily. It was clearly not oh-kay. She took off her green American Eagle cardigan so that they weren't as matchy. "Out of curiosity, who paid for all your Rock & Republic the last time you were here?" she asked accusingly, balling the cardigan up and shoving it in her handsewn plaid purse.

"Look, I'm sorry!" Emily threw up her arms. She'd already had the worst Friday night of her life and wished Paige would just drop it so she could try to enjoy her Saturday. They were going back to Cedartown tomorrow, and Emily wanted one fun L.A. experience that wasn't totally tainted. "I should have told you I came here with Mac. I just didn't want you to get jealous."

"*Jealous*?" Paige screeched, as though she had never heard that word before. Her face turned pink all the way to her ears. "You know what? You have been a total pain ever since you got *discovered*!" Paige shrieked.

A thirtysomething woman in a DKNY T-shirt with her baby in a matching DKNY onesie looked over at them.

"I *was* happy for you when I thought you had the part. At least then I would have spent a week alone with your mom for a *reason*." Paige's frizzy brown hair had frizzed up even more in the balmy L.A. heat. Her brown eyes flashed angrily.

Emily felt like Paige was pouring a concoction of salt and lemon juice into a deep paper cut. She'd been so hurt and embarrassed last night, and she couldn't believe Paige was willfully reminding her of it. "I *knew* you were jealous!" Emily yelled back. "You're probably *happy* that I didn't get that stupid part."

"You should have, because you're officially a drama queen." Paige shook her head disdainfully. "No one made you wear those stupid dresses. Just like no one made you ditch me on this trip." With that, Paige spun on her red Converse All Stars and stormed out of Fred Segal.

Emily walked slowly out of the store and into the parking lot. Behind her, Fred Segal stood with its whimsical red and blue alternating letters and ivy covering. She wished she could crawl into the ivy and disappear.

Paige was right. No one had made her ignore her best friend all week. And no one could magically make everything better.

chapter
TWENTY-SIX

COCO

◄ Saturday　　September 5 ►

8 AM	Wake up
8:01 AM	Try not to freak out (TNTFO)
9:15 AM	Warm up (1 hr)
10:30 PM	Audition for Brigham (really TNTFO)

Coco sat in the lobby of Brigham Powell's West Hollywood office with her mother and Ruby, wearing their Audrey Hepburn–ish outfits, which even Cardammon had to say were "delish."

"Do you want some water?" Ruby asked Coco and Cardammon.

Coco shook her head and held up her SmartWater. Ruby smiled and reached into her duffel for a bottle. If she was thinking about the drama at Kimmie's party last night, she didn't show it.

Coco envied Ruby's calm. Every time she'd try to visualize her dance, Mac's face appeared instead.

The walls of Brigham Powell's L.A. office were exposed red brick, adorned with framed platinum records and pictures of Brigham with all the pretty, polished starlets whose careers he'd created. Miss

Tiara, Hello Cutie, Hug Machine, the Oh-Gees, and of course, Cardammon. Her picture was framed, signed, and the biggest of them all.

Brigham emerged from his office through a steel-gray door. "Babycakes!" he cried, spotting Cardammon. His face had that leathery look of someone who'd remained the same age for several decades thanks to too much tanning/plastic surgery/hair dye. Brigham and Cardammon air-kissed six times.

Mwah mwah mwah mwah mwah mwah!

"And this," Brigham said, holding Coco's face. "I know who this is! Gorgeous!" Coco figured he said that to everyone, but she liked it anyway. She smiled, careful not to show her teeth, à la Cardammon.

"And you must be Ruby?" he said.

Ruby nodded coyly.

"Quite a smashing duo," Brigham said approvingly to Cardammon. His hair was Just For Men–box dark brown, and his eyes were a watery shade of blue.

Ruby and Coco smiled in unison.

"So shall we begin?" he said, waving his left arm for the girls to follow him into the dance studio. The plan was for the girls to dance together to a song Coco had recorded earlier that summer. Brigham wanted to see their "star factor." Everything else, like, well, vocals, could be fixed in postproduction. But what Brigham couldn't fix was panache: Either you had it, or you didn't. Even more important, either you had it *together*, or you didn't. Duos, as Cardammon had explained in the Bentley ride over, were all about chemistry.

"Do you need to take a few minutes to warm up?" Brigham asked the girls, the tanned skin at the corners of his eyes crinkling.

Ruby smiled but shook her head. "Coco and I are good to go, Brigs," she said confidently.

Coco set her black Danskin dance bag down on the wooden floorboards with a thud. *Brigs?*

"Well, that's a new one," Brigham said, looking at Ruby thoughtfully. "Whenever you're ready."

Coco took a deep breath, smiled tightly at her mom and Brigham, and then turned to face the mirrors, Ruby echoing the motion behind her. The opening chords of "Do What I Want" played over the sound system, and she and Ruby spent the next four and a half minutes running through the dance that they'd rehearsed so many times that week.

Coco flung her arms up and shook her hips. "Do What I Want" was a total girl-power song, and their dance moves were a jumble of in-your-face hip-hop moves and ballet leaps with a lot of pointing and winking worked in.

I do what I want

And I want what I do

And baby right now what I want is you

As she listened to her own song lyrics, Coco couldn't help but think of Mac, who always did what she wanted and got what she wanted no matter what it was. Coco felt bad for having lied to her best friend. But then again, she had tried to warn Mac: six calls to her cell, three e-mails, four texts, and two times in person. It wasn't her fault that Mac was unreachable. Mac had been acting downright self-absorbed, and Coco wouldn't have been surprised to find she'd been deliberately ignoring Coco's calls.

Ruby pirouetted by Coco, who remembered to spin, two beats late.

Suddenly the music stopped, and Coco realized her audition was over, and she had no idea how she had gone from the first beat to the last. She'd auditioned on autopilot.

Brigham didn't say anything for nearly ten seconds. Ruby and Coco tried to catch their breath. He looked around the room, from Cardammon, to Coco, to Ruby, and nodded, very slowly.

"Oh my!" Brigham said finally, clearing his throat. His smile was frozen. "Gorgeous!"

"Thanks!" Ruby said, giving a small curtsy.

"Um, Cardammon, may I have a word with you?" Brigham said, nodding his head toward the hallway. "You stay here," he said to Coco and Ruby. "We'll be right back."

Coco emerged from the bathroom, still trying to swallow the knot in her throat. It was a combination of fighting with Mac and just plain nerves. She could hear her mother's and Brigham's voices floating down the exposed brick hallway. She did what any girl would do—she listened.

"Believe me, I wanted them to be the next Cardammon Times Two. We all did." Brigham sighed. "But she needs more time."

"Bollocks!" Cardammon hollered.

Coco leaned against the rough brick of the wall.

"Do you know who is ready to be a pop star? *You.*"

"You're despicable!" Cardammon hissed.

"Am I? Just because I join the rest of the world in wanting you to make another album?"

"I'm done, Brigham. I'm a mother and a fashion designer now. We're not having this conversation again," she said firmly. "I can't believe you took this meeting to try to convince *me* to make another album!"

"Not just you. I'm going to sign Ruby too," he whispered. "But Coco needs a bit more time to live up to Mummy. We don't want her going out under-cooked, do we?"

The lump in Coco's throat swelled. She tried to swallow the tears, but it was too late. A few warm drops fell down her face before she managed a shuddering breath. She couldn't let them see her there, knowing that she'd heard every-thing. It would be too embarrassing for everyone—especially her.

As quietly as possible, Coco tiptoed around the hallway to the side door and back to the dance studio.

"Good job," Coco said softly as she spotted Ruby stretching on the floor. She wiped under her bottom eyelashes, making sure her eyeliner hadn't smeared. "You really nailed it."

"Thanks." Ruby smiled, looking genuinely grate-ful. "Listen, I'm—"

The door opened and Cardammon and Brigham made their way to where the girls were. Ruby stood up eagerly.

"Great job, gorgeous," Brigham said, blinking his blue eyes at Coco. "I want you to stay lovely and train and come see me in six months." Brigham leaned in and gave her a big hug. When they pulled away, Coco wanted to wipe the Brigham off her, but she smiled politely instead.

"And *you*, my dear," he said to Ruby, squeezing her tiny shoulder. "We need to talk."

Ruby's eyes lit up. Coco felt a heavy thud in the pit in her stomach.

"'Bye, Brigham," Cardammon said coldly, picking up her metallic quilted Chanel bag from the floor.

"*Ciao bella*," he said to Cardammon, leaning in for their air-kiss ceremony. She offered her cheek, no *mwah*.

This was serious.

Coco and her mom walked out the door, leaving Ruby to get the good news of her new solo deal. Coco didn't need to hear it twice.

"You were brill, luvvy," Cardammon said, putting her arm around Coco.

Coco cringed, replaying the conversation between her mother and Brigham in her mind. She hated feeling like she'd disappointed her mum. She hated that she'd just helped Ruby Goldman get a major record deal. She hated that on top of all this, her best friend was mad at her.

For the first time in her life, Coco really felt like a solo act.

CHAPTER
TWENTY-SEVEN

mac

◀ Saturday   September 5 ▶

10 AM   Wake up

10:15 AM   Wear pre-selected Cynthia Rowley dress

11 AM   Brunch @ Polo Lounge w/ Mama Armstrong

t was Mac's Saturday to have brunch with her mom at the Polo Lounge in the Beverly Hills Hotel. They were sitting under the twisting hemlock tree that shaded the patio at a white-and-green-tableclothed table. Adrienne had gotten home from New Zealand late last night and had just finished her second latte and third carrot juice. It was a sure-fire jetlag remedy.

Even though Mac was looking adorable in a brand-new Cynthia Rowley sundress, she felt terrible. Her insides twisted and her teeth hurt from clenching her jaw. She'd tossed and turned until dawn, feeling furious at her friends for lying to her last night. Not even the thought of a Polo Lounge Dutch apple pancake could cheer her up.

Mac and her mom's next round of lattes had just arrived when Adrienne's cell phone rang.

"What do you want from me?" Adrienne sighed, as if the phone could answer.

The caller ID read, DAVEY WOODWARD.

Mac leaned into the table, pretending that she had to butter her nine-grain bread. Adrienne pressed the speaker button.

"Hello, hunny!" Adrienne said to the phone as she brought the steaming white mug to her lips. "What's going on? Are you loving your Anastasia?"

Mac craned her neck to hear the voice on the other line. Her bread was getting an insane amount of butter.

"Uhhh, yeah, that's what I wanted to talk to you about," Davey said cautiously.

"Talk to me," Adrienne said, fully alert. She was like a mother bear, fiercely protective and flooded with adrenaline whenever she sensed her clients were in trouble.

"I can't work with Anastasia. She's terrible. She can't act. She has *maybe* one facial expression. I just can't do it. I can't," Davey moaned.

Mac gripped the cushy green-and-white-striped chair, her knuckles white. There was justice in the world, after all. Maybe it wasn't too late for Emily to get the part. Maybe her mom would finally listen to her, and they could call Emily and—

"That may be true, but little girls love her," Adrienne said, dumping Splenda packets into her latte.

"I know . . ." Davey said. "But I really liked your other client." Mac held her breath. *Other client?*

"Other client?" Adrienne asked. She set down her mug.

Mac focused on her heavily buttered roll and tried not to make eye contact.

"Emily-something? She was great," Davey continued. "Really natural. Like I didn't have to act!"

"I just want to be clear that we're talking about the same person," Adrienne said slowly, buying time. Mac knew Adrienne couldn't tell Davey that she had no idea who he was talking about. She'd look like a terrible agent.

"You know, Mac's friend? She was at the audition."

"Of course," Adrienne said, as though she'd understood all along.

And Mac was sure that she *would* understand, just as soon as she got Davey off the phone. Hello, she was Emily's *agent*. *She* found her. Her mom would be so proud.

Adrienne cleared her throat. "Davey, I know it's frustrating, but Anastasia gets butts in seats. They crunched the numbers. . . . When you have kids, this will pay for their houses in Beverly Hills. So if you don't thank me, *they* will. And of course, we'll get Anastasia classes."

"I guess so," Davey relented. "Thanks, Ad."

"Love you, doll," Adrienne said, hanging up the phone. And then she looked at Mac: "Start from the beginning and tell me everything," she said stonily.

". . . so the audition was amazing, and Davey loved Emily," Mac told her mom, smiling brightly just thinking about it. She'd told Adrienne the whole story, from the very start, omitting a few key points, like Erin's performance as the first female partner at Initiative.

As Mac reenacted the slow-clap at the studio, she couldn't help but imagine her own office at Initiative. Her mom would do all the business work, but Mac would be her in-the-field recruiter, finding talent at restaurants and malls, maybe even a few undiscovereds at BAMS. She'd paint her office walls red, and she and her mom would shout things like, "Nice work, Little-Armstrong!" between meetings with their star clients.

"And even *Shane* loved her. So what happens next?" Mac finally finished.

Adrienne crossed her arms and took another sip of latte. She cleared her throat. Mac leaned forward, readying herself for the congratulations that were going to come next. Finally, her mom spoke:

"Davey will learn to work with Anastasia. And I will *not* have a daughter who lies."

Mac's mouth dropped. "You mean you're not going to get Emily the part? You . . . you . . . could just call the producers!"

"Mackenzie!" Adrienne whisper-yelled, "do you expect me to *reward* your dishonesty?"

Mac squared her shoulders and tried to remain calm even though she was definitely not supposed to talk back to her mother. "You're making a huge mistake."

"And *you* are grounded," Adrienne told her daughter calmly, "until I think of a worthwhile punishment."

"Fine." Mac crossed her arms.

"Fine." Adrienne did the same.

Fine.

CHAPTER
TWENTY-EIGHT

becks

◀ Saturday   September 5 ▶

12 PM   Wake up late. SURF!!!

12:01 PM   Find Austin. Take that, Mac!

1 PM   Guess what? More surfing!

Evangelina Becks-Holloway. She liked the sound of that. She smiled when she thought about the sunburned *A* on her back. What else could that mean, except that Austin wanted the world to know she was his? It was the only thing making her smile today, because whenever she remembered the very public fight with her best friend, her stomach felt unsettled, like she'd just drunk an entire carton of whole milk on one of her dad's dares.

Becks put on her cutest Abercrombie white cotton dress and flip-flops, and painted little yellow dots on her toes to look like daisies, just to be extra girly. Then she applied a shimmery layer of Dr Pepper lip gloss. She smelled good and she looked good. She felt like she was channeling her inner Mac, then shook off the thought. She didn't need Mac; she could do this on her own.

Becks headed to the backyard where her dad was loading trash cans for a special stunt. His two buddies from *That Was Clutch*, Stone Matthews and Jack Jackson, were trying to cook omelettes on the grill. They all wore orange Crocs.

"Becks, you do realize the significance of what we're doing today, I hope," Jack said, flipping the eggs in the pan, which sat on the grill. Becks shook her head. All she knew was that there was a perfectly good Wolf range inside and that her dad's pals were going to attempt to run across a row of twenty exploding trash cans, while Clutch, sticking to his retirement promise, filmed away.

"We're essentially running through fire, *if* that fire were balanced on cylinders," Jack said, scratching his mullet. "If it works, we're using it in a reunion movie. But if not, it's a pretty sweet excuse for a barbecue."

"You know your dad's, like, a rare breed, right?" Stone said. His voice always sounded like he'd just woken up. "He's such a live-it-to-the-max dude," he added, looking wistfully out at the Pacific. Becks followed his gaze to the beach and noticed Austin and Boone were already there, playing on his beach blanket.

She tucked her board under her arm and raced

toward Austin's red plaid beach blanket without another word. Through the haze, she saw a shimmer of white on top of the blanket. Was it Mac's brother, Jenner? Becks felt a twinge of disappointment that it wouldn't just be her and Austin, ahem, *alone* this afternoon.

Becks was already thinking of how to tease Austin for putting the *A* on her back. "Do you even know the *ick* drama you caused last night," was the line she planned to use.

But as Becks got closer, she saw that the white blur on top of Austin's blanket was definitely *not* Jenner.

It was Ellie Parker. Ruby Goldman's minion.

Ellie was sprawled with her hands behind her back, her bikini top pointing to the sky, her wavy, dirty-blond hair hanging down so it almost touched the blanket. Becks squeezed the bottom of her board. *What was going on?*

"Becks, you're missing out!" Austin yelled, climbing out of the surf. His body was dripping with water. "The waves are suh-weet!" He retied his Rusty board shorts.

Ellie turned around and smiled at Becks. It took Becks several seconds to stop gawking at her C-cups.

"Um, hi?" Ellie laughed. "How long have you been standing there?"

Okay, so she'd been lurking behind Ellie like a stalker. And she still hadn't answered Austin.

"Hey, Becks, you know Ellie, right?" Austin said.

"Hi," Becks said, the most unenthusiastic *hi* ever.

Ellie curled her fingers in a girly wave. Her arms looked like little tan twigs ready to snap.

"Ellie's going surfing today, too," Austin said. "Right, girl?"

Becks flinched. *Girl?*

"I cannot surf!" Ellie giggled, in the same baby voice as Ruby, and turned to Becks. "Austin's told me how you're like . . . sooooo good."

Austin laughed and shook his sandy brown hair out of his eyes. "Less talking, more surfing!"

Becks took off her pretty white dress, revealing her favorite red-and-white Quiksilver bikini underneath, while Austin and Ellie made their way into the waves. They walked close together, only a foot or two separating them, talking as they walked. Becks grabbed her board and splashed after them, feeling like Boone, not wanting to be left out.

When they were knee-deep in water, Ellie leaned on her board and promptly slipped off. "I can't dooooo this!" she said, laughing, as though it was the cutest thing in the world to fall off a surfboard.

Becks rolled her eyes, waiting for Austin to tell

Ellie he'd see her after he surfed with Becks. The waves were huge and he wasn't going to wait around for Little Miss Slippery-Board to figure out how to climb on. She shot him a glance and tried to catch his blue-gray eyes.

But Austin just smiled and *carried Ellie's board* further into the water, while she bounced behind him.

"Thanks, Austin," Ellie cooed. Her chest was practically her own flotation device, and her back was perfectly tan. And initial-free.

"You got it," Austin turned to wink at Ellie.

Becks felt like she'd swallowed a gallon of seawater. Without saying goodbye, she grabbed her board and dragged it home. It felt heavier than it had all week. They didn't seem to notice she'd left.

"Back already?" Jack asked from his perch at the grill. The omelette was blackened by now. Jack actually owned a T-shirt that read, BURNT IS BETTER.

"Just in time for some homemade wheatgrass juice," Stone said, hoisting a pitcher at Becks.

"I'm gonna shower," Becks said, grateful her voice didn't crack. She could feel the tears fighting their way up from her belly toward her face.

"But you hardly got wet!" Stone called out.

Becks had already sprinted up the stairs to her bedroom to cry in private. She flung herself onto her water bed, wondering how she could have gotten everything so wrong. How could she have been stupid enough to think Austin could like *her*—sporty, awkward, girl-next-door Becks?

Becks needed to feel better, fast. She wanted to call Mac, but that was out of the question. She dialed the next best thing, and then felt guilty for thinking that.

"Hey." Coco's voice sounded almost as hollow as her own through her iPhone.

"Hey." Becks lay back on her bed and glanced at her ocean-floor-blue walls. "Can we still have our sleepover without Mac?" Becks asked, trying to stay composed.

"Hello? Um, of course we don't need Mac to have a sleepover," Coco said matter-of-factly. "Besides, I've never needed it more," she added with a sigh.

Becks nodded and then remembered that Coco couldn't see her.

"I'llseeyoutonightIcan'twait," she said, as fast as she could, trying to hang up the phone before the tears spilled from her eyes. Again.

Chapter
TWENTY-nine

mac

◀ Saturday   September 5 ▶

7 PM   Dinner @ Chateau Marmont w/ girls

7:01 PM   Check to make sure I'm best dressed at resto

7:05 PM   Graciously accept apologies

11 PM   Sleepover chez Becks

Mac arrived at Chateau Marmont at 7 p.m., already on the lookout for her girls. She'd texted them the plan an hour ago, knowing full well they were too awkward to come out and apologize to her on their own. She was still indignant that they'd left her fighting for social survival at Kimmie's party, but Mac prided herself on being the bigger person. Of course she'd give them the chance to explain themselves.

Besides, anything would be better than staying home. Alone.

So she'd simply bribed Erin into ignoring the whole grounding thing and driving her over while her parents were at dinner at Nobu with friends. Grounding was for girls like Emily from Iowa. Girls like Mac were made for poolside dinners. It was a violation of her DNA to sit home by herself.

"You are a party of four, correct, Miss Armstrong?" the maître d' asked, pausing with four menus in his hands. It was against Chateau Marmont policy to seat a party if all the guests weren't there, but Mac Little-Armstrong was a special case.

She nodded. "I'm a little early, Vigo. But there'll be four of us."

Vigo nodded. "Right this way," he said, leading Mac to her usual table in the back corner of the garden. Mac ordered a virgin Bellini and waited for Coco, Becks, and Emily. She felt badly about what had happened with Emily last night, especially now that her mom wouldn't help her. The least she could do was buy her almost-star a nice meal before she left L.A. for good.

She saw Jessica Simpson at one table and the filmmaker David Lynch across the patio. Next to her a young couple was clearly on a third date, practically rubbing noses.

Minutes passed, and Mac had to stop herself from checking her phone a fifth time for a missed text. There were few things in life that Mac hated more than an untexted phone. She'd been textless for seventeen hours.

"The rest of your party is definitely coming, correct?" Vigo asked. Mac nodded and ordered another virgin Bellini and a pistachio-encrusted goat cheese appetizer.

She sent a quick WHERE R U text to all three girls and then tried to focus on enjoying the Chateau. Emily was probably just lost, but she didn't get how Becks and Coco could be so late for dinner. Or how they could have dismissed the importance of *social chair*, the most important position in the entire school and in Mac's entire life. Or how they could have lied to her. Maybe they were just busy planning an elaborate apology?

Vigo appeared again. "Pardon me, Miss Little-Armstrong." He cleared his throat. "But might I move you over there?" He motioned to a lonely table in the shady corner, facing the wall. "We need this table for a larger party."

Mac was about to say, *But my friends will be here soon.* Then she looked at her watch and realized it was 7:32. Everyone in Hollywood knew that more than half an hour late meant no-show.

She nodded and pushed her chair behind her, knocking her Lanvin Oulala clutch on the ground. As she crawled under the table to retrieve the black suede purse, her emotions tumbled out like her credit cards, strewn over the Chateau Marmont patio.

She'd thought her mom would be proud of her

for finding Emily. She'd thought the Inner Circle was stronger than a Cartier Love bracelet. She'd though that eighth grade was going to be the Best Year Ever.

And now it looked like it was bye-bye BYE.

A tiny, quiet sob escaped her lips before she could stand. And then she couldn't stop. The tears cascaded down her face. Other diners turned to look.

Finally, the maître d' lifted her up and escorted her into the waiting area by the fireplace so she wouldn't disturb the other diners. Normally Mac would have been mortified, but the pain of losing her friends hurt way more than any embarrassment over PDE.

Through sniffles, she texted Erin to come pick her up. Then, even though it was late at night, she put on her Gucci aviators and tried to shut out the world.

For once, Mac Little-Armstrong had zero hope.

CHAPTER THIRTY

Emily's L.A. Itinerary

Saturday, September 5

2 PM Drive to see stars' homes (sit on opposite side of car from Paige)

5:30 PM Dinner at TGIF (sit on opposite side of table as Paige)

7 PM Pack for early-morning flight (at least hiding new clothes is no longer necessary)

Emily was back at the Econo Lodge on Saturday evening packing her red canvas suitcase and listening to the sound of her mother snoring. Paige was taking a shower before bed. She had been keeping her distance and hadn't spoken a word to Emily since their fight at Fred Segal this morning.

The muggy light crept through the blinds, and Emily realized it was almost 7 p.m. Mac would be at Chateau Marmont right about now.

She taped a note on the TV.

Sorry! Last-minute stuff. xoxoxo, E.

She shuddered, knowing how angry her mom and Paige would be to find that super-vague message, but at least that way they wouldn't call the police. It would buy Emily just enough time.

She raced down to Hollywood Boulevard to hail a cab. She had never been in one by herself. It smelled like asparagus and cigarettes, but she barely had time to notice. Her biggest concern was that she'd be too late.

"Would you please wait here?" Emily asked the cabdriver when he stopped in front of the ivy-covered walls.

"You got five minutes," he barked. "And then I'm outta here."

"Got it!" she said, racing to the doors.

She only had a few minutes until Fred Segal closed. It was a simple plan: She'd buy a vintage tee for Paige, head back to the hotel, and win her friend back.

The first person she saw inside the store was Marianne. This time she was wearing a black jump-suit with a tiny white tee underneath and little space-age booties. When Marianne spotted Emily, she smiled. Then, clearly remembering their last encounter, she went right back to her folding.

"Marianne, hi. Please help me. I need to do a major friendship fix," Emily said. "Do you have those special vintage tees? The ones you can only get at *this* store."

"Come with me," Marianne said, leading her to a rack lined with softee tees.

Emily reached for the smallest one. It was a simple

chocolate brown (Paige's best color) scoop
best style), in super-soft cotton, with swir
that said, I'M THE BFF. It was *perfect* for Paige
could hardly believe it. Maybe she'd been su
sciously putting her desires into the universe i
cab ride over.

"Thanks!" Emily threw her arms out and env
oped Marianne in a tight hug. "And by the way, I'n
going back to Iowa but it was great meeting you!"
she cried as she raced to the cashier.

Marianne looked stunned but gave a wave as Emily used every cent of her babysitting money and then darted back into the bad-smelling cab.

Back at the Econo Lodge, Emily found Paige and Lori sitting on the edge of the double beds. The television was on, but no one was paying attention to *Entertainment Tonight*. They glared when Emily entered.

"You left while I was napping, *without telling me where you were going*," Lori said, her arms crossed over her chest. Paige looked down at her water glass. On the TV screen, Mary Hart excitedly shook hands with Jennifer Lopez, marveling at her four-inch wedges.

"I'm sorry, but I had to get this for Paige," Emily

said, pulling out the white bag with the trademark blue lettering.

Paige took the bag and looked cautiously at her friend.

Emily moved to the center of the room, turned the TV off, and stood in front of it, facing her mom and Paige. She took a deep breath. "Look, you guys, I've been a pain this whole week," she said. She twirled her BFF bangle around her wrist. "I didn't spend any time with you on this trip, I missed out on a lot, and I'm sorry."

Paige opened the bag and pulled out the tee. It was quiet for a moment, the only sound the cars outside.

"It's perfect," she breathed, pulling the soft chocolate-colored fabric into her chest. She lifted her head and smiled at Emily.

"That *is* nice," Lori agreed, looking pointedly at Emily. Her brown eyes were soft.

Just then Emily's phone buzzed. She glanced down, rolled her eyes, and hit the ignore button.

"Mac?" Paige asked. "You can get it. I don't mind."

"That's text number three and call number four tonight," Emily said, rubbing her foot on the brown-flecked carpet.

"It sounds like she wants to talk to you," Paige said.

"Yeah, maybe. But I never want to hear from her again." Emily turned off her phone.

Paige arched her eyebrows as though she wasn't quite sure she believed Emily. Just then their hotel phone began to ring. No one made a move to answer it.

Emily flopped down on the double bed next to Paige, thinking a hotel bed had never felt more comfortable. She grabbed the remote and turned the TV back on to *Entertainment Tonight*.

"This is how Hollywood was meant to be experienced," Emily said, lying on her stomach and resting her head on her hands. Paige grinned and lay down next to her, and Lori settled into the other bed with *The Secret*, smiling.

Tomorrow, they'd be back in Iowa, and Emily would never, ever forget the people who really mattered.

CHAPTER
THIRTY-ONE

becks

◀ Saturday   September 5 ▶

7 PM   Evening—I have plans

10 PM   Nighttime—Figure out how to un-sync phone

Coco and Becks were lounging in Becks's screening room, dressed in their Victoria's Secret Pink pajamas as they ate chocolate-chip cookie dough straight from the tube and microwaveable popcorn. It would have been a very typical, and very perfect, Saturday night sleepover, but both girls knew without saying it that there was one thing missing.

"I can't believe I bombed my audition," Coco said, dipping her hand mindlessly into the popcorn bowl. Madonna was nestled into the couch next to her, her smooshed face looking mournful.

"I can't believe I missed that Austin liked Ellie," Becks said. She lay on her back, her hands behind her head, ready to do crunches.

"Can we watch a movie?" Coco asked. "Preferably one that's not about dancing."

"Or about love," Becks said flatly. "But it's *Mac's* job to bring the movies."

The name *Mac* lingered in the air like tacky vanilla perfume.

That night the girls had followed their usual sleepover ritual: They'd leafed through fashion magazines and made a list of possible buys. They'd done each other's makeup and painted their toenails. (Becks had gone from cute yellow dots that looked like daisies to an ominous shade of black.) They'd even dressed Madonna up in one of Clutch's colorful handkerchiefs. It was all *fun*, and yet, they weren't having fun.

"Does this mean Ruby's gonna be social chair?" Becks asked, getting up from her sleeping bag to sprawl on one of the red velvet couches.

"Probably," Coco said, taking a spoonful of cookie dough and dotting it with popcorn before she put the whole glob into her mouth.

"This year won't be that bad. . . ." Becks began, but she couldn't come up with a reason to back up her point. "Ruby is such a user," she offered instead. "She came to *your* audition and stole *your* deal."

"Yeah, I guess." Coco shrugged. "The thing is, she was really good. Like, so good that I can only be mad at myself." Madonna rubbed her nose against Coco's pajamaed leg for moral support.

"But her stupid friend stole my boy," Becks said bitterly. She stood from the couch, unable to sit still, and started pacing back and forth. "I need a dartboard with her face on it."

"I need cookie dough," Coco said, reaching for another spoonful.

But what both girls really needed was Mac.

CHAPTER THIRTY-TWO

mac

◀ Sunday   September 6 ▶

10 AM   Wake up

10:14 AM   Send Becks polite note explaining how
to un-sync phones?

10:15 AM   Make a list of possible new friends?
GET HAPPY

11 AM   Plan back-to-school ensemble.
GET HAPPY PART DEUX

After finally falling asleep following her embarrassing meltdown at Chateau Marmont, Mac was unprepared for her mother to barge in in the middle of the night. Well, technically it wasn't the middle of the night—it was 7 a.m.

But close enough.

"Rise and shine," Adrienne said in a stern voice. Mac and her mother hadn't spoken since the Great Polo Lounge Blowup. And now here she was, hovering over Mac's bed, ordering her to get up in the wee hours of the morning.

Mac wondered if Erin had spilled about her dinner at Chateau last night. Or about pretending to be Adrienne. Mac imagined she was being sent to a scary get-your-child-in-line boarding school in Utah. This was exactly how it happened on those

TV specials. They barged into your room in the dark and kidnapped you.

"You're not sending me away, are you?" Mac asked, peeking out from her white-and-gold silk fleur-de-lis bedspread.

"Mac. I watched the reel," Adrienne said.

Mac sat up instantly in her four-poster bed, her exhaustion immediately forgotten. "You saw Emily's audition?" she gasped.

"Yes. She *is* talented."

Mac smiled. It was what she had been trying to tell her mother all along. If she could just see this girl act, then she would know she had *It*. "But if she's so good, why didn't she get the part?"

"They didn't want to go with an unknown," Adrienne said simply.

Mac shook out her sleep-messy blond hair. "But what about talent?"

"Mackenzie Marie Little-Armstrong," Adrienne looked right at her daughter. She would have seemed far sterner if she weren't still wearing her red fuzzy slippers. "If you are going to work in this town, and I think you will, remember this: It's not *just* about talent—it's what you do with it. That's lesson number one."

"I never should have lied to you," Mac said.

Adrienne sighed. "You're my daughter. We do whatever it takes for our clients." She shook her head. "*Whatever* it takes. But that doesn't mean you should lie."

"Mom," Mac whispered. "Her flight leaves at 8:45."

"Well . . ." Adrienne paused, examining her red fuzzy slippers. "We're not gonna lose her a second time. Let's go."

THIRTY-THREE

Emily & Paige's L.A. Itinerary

Sunday, September 6

6:00 AM   Wake-up call

7:00 AM   Cab to LAX

8:45 AM   Back to Iowa (can't wait)

E mily zipped her black Forever 21 hoodie up to her chin. It was 7:20 a.m. in Los Angeles and the sky was a dull gray color, the occasional gust of wind making it chilly for the first time during their trip. Emily closed her eyes and thought of blue skies, grassy fields, dairy cows, and *friendly, normal people* that awaited them on the other side of this flight. Even the Cedartown mall would feel like home after being here.

"Can I take your bags, ma'am?" the American Airlines curbside check-in guys asked Lori.

She shook her head. "Soon," she told him, as if that made any sense at all. Who wanted to hold on to their luggage at the airport?

Then, just when Emily thought they'd maxed out on weirdness for the morning, she noticed a silver Prius at the curb. The door opened, and a girl wearing Victoria's Secret Pink pajamas got out and ran toward the curb, her long golden-blond hair fluttering behind her—Mac!

Mac's smile was so huge that for a second Emily forgot their friendship was over. Emily's jaw dropped. So did Paige's. The two best friends looked at each other, wondering what other last-minute surprises Los Angeles/the universe had brewing. Lori didn't seem surprised at all and winked at the curbside check-in guy.

And then, bounding out of the illegally parked Prius, still wearing her red fluffy slippers, was the real Adrienne Little-Armstrong.

As they approached, Adrienne walked over to Lori. "I'm Adrienne Little-Armstrong," she said, holding out her palm.

"But—" Lori started to gasp.

"As I said on the phone, I think your daughter is phenomenally talented," Adrienne said to Lori, who was still clearly taken aback by Adrienne's shape-shifting. "Do you have some time before the plane takes off?" Adrienne asked.

Mac grabbed Emily's arm. "I know you're mad at me, but hear me out," Mac said, breathlessly. "My mom saw your reel! She wants to represent you."

Emily's leg began to twitch in nervous excitement, but she reminded herself that she'd already been burned by this girl. More like scorched.

"Emily, we're going to make you a star," Mac said. She held out a small pastel-pink gift bag.

Emily looked at Mac, not sure whether to take the peace offering. She'd already heard that star line once before. But Mac was looking at her with such vulnerable, eager hope in her makeup-free eyes, her blond hair whipping messily in the chilly early-morning wind. Emily knew that Mackenzie Little-Armstrong wouldn't be seen in public in her pajamas for just anything, or anyone.

Emily took the bag from Mac's extended hand. Inside was an iPhone.

"We're going to need to reach you twenty-four-seven." Mac grinned.

"I promise I'll pick up." Emily grinned back.

"My best friend is going to be a star!" Paige yelled, bear-hugging Emily. They jumped up and down on the curb of LAX as the other tired travelers turned to look. Emily grabbed Mac and pulled her into the hug.

"It's just going to take me a *leeeetle* longer than a week," Mac said as they pulled apart. "You said it yourself—there's always next time."

Emily smiled. She was just glad there was going to *be* a next time.

CHAPTER
THIRTY-FOUR

mac

◀ Sunday   September 6 ▶

9 AM   GET MY FRIENDS BACK!

"No wonder Erin always looks so exhausted," Adrienne said as she drove Emily and Mac to Malibu. "This is a very long drive." She parked the Prius in front of the Becks family's garage.

"Speaking of Erin," Mac began tentatively, "I sort of promised we'd go to one of her concerts." She reached for the door handle to make a hasty exit.

"Now you're *really* grounded," Adrienne replied, but she was smiling.

"I love you," Mac said innocently, blowing her mom an air kiss.

Adrienne pantomimed catching it midair. "Love you back."

Mac clutched a bag of Winchell's donuts as she and Emily timidly let themselves into the sprawling stucco beach house through Becks's back door.

When they slipped quietly into the screening room, Coco's French bulldog, Madonna, snarled at Mac. *Grrrrr.* Empty packages of Nestlé Toll House cookie dough and Paul Newman's microwave popcorn littered the floor.

"Mac?" Coco asked, sitting up and rubbing her eyes. "Why are you here so early?" Madonna jumped up and sat on Coco's lap protectively.

"Yeah, Mac, why are you here?" Becks asked, her strawberry-blond hair plastered to her cheek. She sounded more surprised than mad.

Mac sighed. She walked over to one of the screening room refrigerators and took out a large bottle of Orangina, pouring it into four champagne flutes. Emily took a seat on the couch behind Coco and Becks.

"And why are you here, Emily?" Coco asked, sounding extra-confused. "Weren't you leaving this morning?"

"We had an impromptu meeting at the airport this a.m. Mama Armstrong saw the tape and is going to rep Emily, who's living with me for a little while, until her mother can move out from Iowa," Mac quickly explained. She had to get down to the business at hand.

Mac sat down on the couch next to Coco. Madonna licked her hand tentatively. "I'm so sorry I wasn't there for you last week. You tried to tell me so many times and I was super MIA. It's great that you're dancing with Ruby—"

"*Was* dancing with Ruby," Coco interrupted, frowning. "I didn't get the deal with Brigham. Ruby did. A *solo* deal. Apparently the only thing wrong with our duet was *me*."

"Well, you dodged that bullet!" Mac said, jumping up from the couch and startling Madonna. "She'll burn out and you'll twinkle forever. She'll be Britney and you'll be Xtina," Mac said, handing a glass of Orangina to each of the girls.

"And Becks." Mac pivoted to face her other BFF. "Why didn't you just tell me you liked Austin?"

"You called him Ruf-Ruf," Becks said flatly. "I thought you thought he was a total loser."

"Better him than Jenner," Mac said flatly, and peered into the box of donuts. She pulled out a chocolate cruller.

"Well, it doesn't matter anyway." Becks shrugged "He's with Ruby's newest follower, Ellie, now."

"Oh, pshaw," Mac said, ripping a piece of donut with her teeth. "We'll get you Austin. I mean, if that's what you want. And Coco, we'll make Ruby sorry she ever put on a leotard." Then Mac turned to Emily. "And Emily, *you* are going to be the next big thing."

"Actually," Emily said slowly, "since I'm new in town, I'd also kind of like . . . a friend. *Or two*," she added, looking shyly at Becks and Coco through her fringe of cinnamon-brown bangs.

"Deal." Coco and Becks nodded in unison.

"Me too," Mac agreed. "I'm just your friend who takes 10 percent." She winked.

"And you, Mac Little-A," Coco said, getting up from the velvet couch, "are going to be social chair!"

Mac beamed at the Inner Circle, which had expanded to four, feeling so overjoyed she just might burst.

She had her friends. She had her talent. School started tomorrow, and it was going to be the Best Year Ever. *Hello, BYE!*

acknowleDGments

Thank you to the talented Joelle Hobeika, Sara Shandler, and Josh Bank for their encouragement and impeccable taste, and to Andrea C. Uva for making it all look wonderful. Thanks to Ben Schrank, Lexa Hillyer, and Jessica Rothenberg for embracing this book and making it bloom. I am extremely grateful to Ruby Boyd for sharing her stories and smarts. I'm also grateful to Vikki Karan for her managerial skills, Joanna Schochet for her advice and funny, Tracey Nyberg for her sharp eye and studio space, and Kyle Vannatter for his good luck. Christina Passariello, Helene Fouquet, Emilie Boyer King, Katrin Bennhold, Rachel Tiplady, Abby Stern, Stephanie Oswald, Hillary Biscay, Lisa Harrison, Catherine Sugar, Amee McNaughton, and Les Plesko very kindly shared their support and savvy. And to Alyse, George, and Colleen Shaw—thank you for everything, and especially for keeping the faith.

It's going to be the BYE for the IC—or is it?
Find out in . . .

ZOEY DEAN'S
TALENT
ALMOST FAMOUS

Mac's life is *almost* perfect. She discovered an *almost–* movie star, and she's almost sealed the deal on Social Chair. But in Hollywod, *almost* doesn't cut it. And nobody knows that better than Ruby Goldman, whose only wish is to see Mac and her friends go from *almost there* to *completely over*. When Ruby gets her petal-pink fingernails on some embarrassing gossip about the Inner Circle, her wish just might come true. It's up to Mac to make sure their BYE doesn't go buh-bye . . .

TALENT
YOU EITHER HAVE IT OR YOU DON'T

DO YOU HAVE IT?
Prizes, quizzes, contests, and blogs at www.zoeydeanstalent.com

ZOEY DEAN'S
TALENT

It's not just a book.
It's the search for the next big star!

Enter Zoey Dean's Talent Contest.
Audition online & show off your talent.

You could win a trip to LA,
meet with a Hollywood casting director
& get discovered!

To enter, & for official rules, go to
www.sugarloot.com/besttalent or **www.zoeydeanstalent.com**

When it comes to TALENT,
you either have it or you don't.